W9-BSA-320

SERILDA'S STAR

She put the chain around Serilda's neck

SERILDA'S STAR

by

OLIVE RAMBO COOK

Illustrated by HELEN TORREY

LONGMANS, GREEN AND CO.

NEW YORK · LONDON · TORONTO

1959

LONGMANS, GREEN AND CO., INC.
119 WEST 40TH STREET, NEW YORK 18

LONGMANS, GREEN AND CO., LTD.
6 & 7 CLIFFORD STREET, LONDON W 1

LONGMANS, GREEN AND CO.
20 CRANFIELD ROAD, TORONTO 16

SERILDA'S STAR

PUBLISHED SIMULTANEOUSLY IN THE DOMINION OF CANADA BY
LONGMANS, GREEN AND CO., TORONTO

FIRST EDITION

LIBRARY OF CONGRESS CATALOG CARD NUMBER 59–12747

Printed in the United States of America

To
the memory of
my mother and father
EFFIE M. and GEORGE W. RAMBO
who both loved horses

Acknowledgments

For their help the author is grateful to the following persons of
Chillicothe, Missouri:

Mrs. Earl Dupy, who lived near the bridge when a little girl, and
let me use her lovely name—Serilda

Elmer Goben,* for information and scale drawings of the bridge

Mrs. Edgar Reynolds

Mrs. George Van Deventer

Mrs. James L. Francis

Miss Clyta Anderson

Miss Persis Meek

Mrs. David Girdner

Joseph D. Stewart

Oscar Darr*

Mrs. Mike Girdner*

Goodlou Grouse,* for facts about the bridge opening ceremony

Mrs. Ethel Randolph*

Mose Hutchinson*

Fred Gunby, for access to old county maps

The Chillicothe Chamber of Commerce

The Librarians of Livingston County Memorial Library

And for the Centennial Edition of the *Chillicothe Constitution-
Tribune,* published September 13, 1937

Also to:

Mrs. John L. Brooks,* My Aunt Lena of Kansas City, Missouri,
who lived to be 94 and told me much about the early days

Guy H. Stone, Monett, Missouri, for facts and drawings of the
forebay

*deceased

[ix]

ACKNOWLEDGMENTS

Mrs. S. M. Solomon, Carthage, Missouri, for the use of the History of Caldwell and Livingston Counties, compiled by early settlers and the St. Louis National Historical Society, 1886

Melissa and Paul Shaw, Auburn, Alabama

Miss Jane Palmer, Editor of *Wee Wisdom,* Lee's Summit, Missouri, who published part of Serilda's Star as two serials

Miss May Brookshier, Houston, Texas

Mrs. Walter Pondrom, Jr., and Vicki Pondrom, Houston, Texas

W. A. Lawson, Westmoreland Stables, Houston, Texas

Sandy Whitehill, Whitehill Stables, Houston, Texas, for permission to use the name Radiant Star

Miss Gerry Stockton, Children's Librarian, Austin Public Library, Austin, Texas.

The Librarians of Bellaire Community Library, Bellaire, Texas, and the Main Public Library, Houston, Texas

And many, many others

Illustrations

She put the chain around Serilda's neck

Frontispiece

Page

As if she were high above the world   5

It's as if we knew each other, Serilda thought   15

The stallion was running ahead, clearing the
road for them   61

They had crossed the bridge   83

"Here they come. Pa's leadin' the line!"   101

Katie read the whole lesson   125

"Star, my Star! You're found!"   147

SERILDA'S STAR

CHAPTER 1

On a High Hill

SERILDA SHAW ran up the path from the log house, brown braids swinging, pantalets swishing against her ankles, and full skirts flying out behind. Grover, the tan-and-white shepherd dog, raced ahead, leading the way to the pasture where the big, flat rock jutted out from the high hill.

Serilda swung up on the rock. Standing slim and straight, she shaded her eyes from the afternoon sun and looked to the northwest, trying to follow the road that wound across Grand River Valley to the village of Spring Hill. Early that morning Pa and her brother, Jeff, had left for the sawmill near the village for a load of timbers for the new bridge. She watched for the tiny moving spot that would be the big bay horses, Tib and Tony, and behind them, hauling the second load, the double yoke of oxen. But there was no sight of them.

Serilda sighed impatiently and sat down. Maybe Pa had trouble with the new team. She had been to the mill with Jeff and Pa. Just thinking of the shrill scream of the big saw ripping through the logs made a shiver down her back. She could almost smell the

[1]

sharp, pungent odor of the fresh sawdust and hear the slap-slap of the wide leather band as it slithered from the puffing engine to the saw. Full of strange noises, it was a worrisome place for horses.

But Pa could handle any horse, Serilda thought proudly. Even the fine new team that seemed so gentle but was strong and powerful.

There was an ache in Serilda's heart when she thought of the new team, for Pa had traded two yoke of oxen and their horse, Coaly, for the big bay Percherons brought from the East. "I don't care how fine they are, I'm not going to love them," Serilda promised herself when she found out Pa had taken Coaly away without a good-by or a last bite of apple. He said it was better to do it that way; but there was a lonely, resentful feeling every time she thought of shiny, black Coaly. Coaly, who willingly pulled them to school in the old buggy they had found wrecked and Pa had mended.

It did not help when Pa explained that he would use the horses to haul lumber for the bridge. With the extra money he would help to build a new house. They could buy another horse later, but the ache was still there.

Grover suddenly looked toward the road, a soft rumble in his throat. Serilda looked, too; then she jumped to her feet, eyes shining. It was Colonel Thompson on Black Chief, the stallion! She watched spellbound as the stallion went by. Head held high, long black tail rippling out behind, black legs flashing, he was all motion and grace, so sleek and handsome he fairly took one's breath. Oh, for a horse like that!

Often the Colonel passed from his home near Chillicothe going to his son's farm across the river. Pa said the stallion was a registered thoroughbred and Colonel Thompson had the papers to prove it locked up in a tin box in the bank.

Serilda watched until the horse and rider went out of sight. Then she gave a deep sigh and sat down again. She ran her fingers through the thick hair on Grover's neck, and a determined look came on her round face. "Remember what I say, Grover. Sometime I'll have me a horse of my very own—a fine, high-stepping one like Colonel Thompson's thoroughbred. And no one is going to take him away from me. I'll keep him forever and ever."

Grover wrinkled his forehead and looked so puzzled at Serilda that she burst out laughing.

Up here on the high rock, Serilda always felt as if she were high above the world with a giant colored map spread before her. Today the map was as bright as a piecework quilt, for it was October, 1866, in northern Missouri, and the rolling hills and valleys were brilliant with the red and yellow of autumn leaves.

[3]

To the west, reaching up against the sky, was the Knob, highest of all the hills. Far across the valley to the north was the blue of Indian Hill. Pa could remember when Indians had a village there. Sometimes bands of them still came through and camped down by the river. Serilda's eyes followed the shine of Grand River as it flowed in from the northeast, making a bend at the foot of the hill as it turned to the west. The bend of the river was the part of the map that she loved best. Here she could see where the new covered bridge was being built, and, a short way upstream, Amos Carter's ferry. She could see the ferry now, moving slowly across the river carrying a team and wagon and Colonel Thompson on the black stallion.

She could not see Amos Carter's house, where he lived alone, even though it was within yelling distance of the ferry, nor could she see the Dentons' home farther east; but she could see parts of the road that led past the Dentons' to Red Oaks school.

Plainest of all the marks on the map were the white limestone abutments for the new bridge, one on each side of the river. Grandma said there had been another bridge built across the river at this site in 1843, but it had burned and since then there had been a ferry.

By the ferry was a camp site, a cleared place on this side of the river where campers had cut down

As if she were high above the world

trees for firewood. Handy to the river and the ferry, movers in their covered wagons, with horses and cattle straggling behind, stopped here to rest.

Serilda tried to think how it would seem to be a mover, without a home and with everything you owned in a wagon or walking along behind it. But she shook her head and gave up the idea, for Grandpa had come overland from Indiana and settled this land and built the log house and lived here the rest of his life. And Pa was born here; eleven years ago she was born here. A year later Jeff was born, and this spring little Bill. She could not imagine living in a covered wagon.

Serilda felt as if she knew every rock and board that was going into the bridge, for Jeff talked about nothing else. He knew where every piece of timber that he and Pa had hauled from the mill was to be used. Big, friendly Steven Ambrose, builder of the bridge, had shown Jeff the patterns and he had almost memorized them.

Jeff knew, too, exactly what he was going to do when he grew up. He was going to build bridges, long ones that reached across wide rivers. Serilda puzzled a little, wondering what she would be doing. Whatever it was, there would be horses in it—fine, swift, high-stepping horses. Of that Serilda was perfectly sure.

She looked down into the yard at the gray weathered house with the grapevines growing on a trellis by the back door. There was the rounded, grassy mound of the cave, with the slanting wooden door in the side that little Bill loved to play on. There were steps that led down to an inside door that opened into a small rock-walled room where vegetables and fruit were stored for the winter, and butter and milk kept in the summer. Serilda's mouth watered, thinking of the apples that stayed firm and juicy almost until apple time again. Twice, when fierce black storm clouds turned day into night, they had gone to the cave for safety, all but Grandma, who refused to go.

There was the high wellcurb and windlass where you let down a bucket on a rope and drew up cool water from the well. Serilda gave a little sigh of thankfulness for the well, for many of the neighbors carried water from a spring half a mile or more from their house.

Grandma Shaw was sitting on the back step, little Bill crawling around her feet. Ma was taking in the washing from the line, folding an extra quilt which had been drying on the rail fence. Ma never stopped working, and Serilda felt a twinge of guilt, coming up to the high rock just for pure pleasure.

She glanced back across the valley, shaded her eyes again, then leaned forward intently as a moving dark spot came in sight nearly a mile away. She watched for a minute, then she bounded from the rock and raced for the house, Grover tearing along beside her.

"Ma! I see Pa and Jeff coming. Can I go meet 'em and watch 'em unload the big timbers? I'll take 'em a cool drink. They'll be awful thirsty. Can I, Ma?"

Serilda stood breathless, waiting, her blue eyes entreating.

Ma gave a little sigh. "Serilda, won't you ever learn to act like a lady? You may go, but don't run all the way down the hill, or there will not be a drop of water in the bucket when you get there. Remember what happened the last time?"

"I'll get the one with a lid," Serilda said, and flew into the house and came back with a small tin bucket. Quickly she drew water from the well and hurried out to the road. She walked as fast as she could without running, holding the bucket out stiffly beside her.

CHAPTER 2

Serilda and Amos Pilot the Ferryboat

AMOS CARTER was down at the ferry getting ready to go across. "Step lively and you can take it over," he called out. "Time for your Pa and Jeff, and I want to be on hand when they unload the big timbers. Guess you're hankerin' to see that, too." His face was lean and weathered, but his eyes were friendly and he smiled at Serilda, the smile partly hidden by a little brown mustache and a scraggly set of chin whiskers.

Serilda ran down the steep road and on to the ferry, her eyes shining. She set the tin bucket down carefully, then hurried to her place by the trolley rope. Amos had lately taught her how to guide the ferry.

There was a thick rope cable stretched across the river, fastened securely at each end to heavy posts set deep in the bank on either side. Wooden pulleys, that ran on the cable, with trolley ropes fastened to each end of the ferry, kept the course straight as the current propelled one across the river. When the river was high and the current strong, they went across in a hurry, but when it was low, as it was now, you drifted across so gently you hardly knew you were moving.

Amos tugged at the rope that pulled up the south apron of the ferry, gave it a quick hitch around the bannister, and came to stand by Serilda. "Let her out," he said crisply.

Serilda unwrapped the near trolley rope from its wooden button and let it lengthen a few feet. The end of the ferry began drifting down the stream, then the current caught it and began pushing it across the river. Serilda gave a quick twist to the rope and fastened it securely.

Amos nodded approvingly and leaned against the bannister. "Only two times I showed you and you've done it perfectly. If you were a boy you'd make a good hand."

Serilda's face flushed with pleasure. Then a thoughtful look came into her eyes. "Amos, why shouldn't a lady ride fast horses and pilot a ferryboat and swim in the river and hunt bee trees?"

Amos scratched his chin and looked at the far bank. "I guess she could, Serilda, but most ladies don't. Someway it just don't seem fittin'. And anyway, with all the cookin' and cleanin' and weavin' and spinnin' and baby tendin', there ain't time to do them things 'cept when you're growin' up."

Serilda sighed. "Then I wish I didn't ever have to grow up."

Amos snorted. "After forty years, you'd get awful tired of bein' a young'un!"

Serilda laughed. She liked Amos. He was good to children, letting them ride across the ferry without paying, unless it was a special trip. And now that Pa and Jeff were hauling for the bridge he let the Shaws cross on the ferry for almost nothing.

As they neared the bank, Amos let down the north apron of the ferry with a clatter and tied the ferry to the post, while Serilda pulled up the slack she had let out in the trolley rope and fastened it to the button.

She picked up the bucket of water and with Amos walked up the slope to the main road and waited near the unloading place.

Down the road Pa and Jeff were just coming into sight. Jeff was ahead, standing up on the load like a grown man, driving the big bays, Tib and Tony. Blond hair curling out from under his cap, blue eyes in a tanned face—he was a fine sight. He guided the team expertly to the stopping place and jumped down from the wagon, a grin spreading across his dusty, sweat-stained face when he saw his sister.

Serilda took off the lid of the bucket and he lifted it up and drank his fill. "It sure tastes good," he said with a gusty sigh.

Jeff looked at the horses and then at the long, foot-square, white oak timbers chained on the running gears of the wagon.

[11]

"Lacked half a mile going to the sawmill today," Jeff said, "and Tib and Tony must be glad. These timbers are too big for the mill to handle, so they're hewed out by hand. And Pa let me drive Tib and Tony half the way. Not another team in the county could haul three of these oak cords up and down hill for five miles. Takes some pulling, I tell you. Eighteen feet long and Pa says he reckons the load close to a ton and a half."

Serilda looked at the big horses with grudging admiration. She reached out and rubbed Tony's sweating face. "How many is Pa hauling?"

"Two, and that's a big load for two yoke of oxen. And there's nine more of these big fellers ready and waiting."

There was the squeak of wheels and a little cloud of dust as Pa, driving the two yoke of oxen, came slowly along. Serilda felt a surge of pure happiness as she watched the tall, dark-haired man coming toward them, his blue shirt open at the neck and his brown linsey-woolsey pants tucked into high leather boots. He walked proud like, his tall body swinging along beside the brindle oxen. Serilda knew there was a twinkle in his brown eyes.

Serilda hurried to offer the cool water. Pa smiled gratefully. "I was just plumb dried out," he said after the second drink. "Guess you talked your ma into coming down to see us unload," he said teasingly.

"Well, you watch and you'll really see things move."

Pa went over to Tib and Tony, loosened the doubletree from the wagon, and drove them around to the back. There, he looped a chain around a timber, fastened it to the doubletree, and gave the signal. The big bays bowed their necks, leaned forward, and walked the big timber right off the wagon to a spot near the abutment.

Amos Carter came close to watch and the bridge men stopped working, too. Serilda could feel Pa's pride as he guided the fine Percherons. She almost, but not quite, forgave Pa for selling Coaly to help buy them.

Suddenly Jeff nudged Serilda, his eyes shining. He pointed to the north abutment near them. "Look! They've started the falsework. See the two poles standing up in the water on each side? Mr. Ambrose said they shove the poles clean down into the bottom of the river and nail braces crosswise and lengthwise and put boards across like a floor. That's where the men stand to work, and it holds up the real bridge until they get it fixed solid." He grinned importantly.

Serilda laughed. "You know, I believe you could build a bridge right now if you had to." Jeff didn't answer but there was a pleased look on his face.

When the unloading was finished, Jeff and Serilda went across the ferry with the oxen and the empty wagon. As they came up the bank, Serilda saw a covered wagon coming down the long hill. "Movers," she said to Jeff in an excited voice. "Do you think they'll cross the ferry or stop at the camp site?"

They waited for Pa to cross the ferry and watched as the covered wagon came nearer. It passed in front of them and turned into the campground.

A man and a woman were on the front seat, the woman's face thin and pale under her limp sunbonnet. She held a baby in her arms and two small boys peered over her shoulders. The man was heavy and red-faced, with a slouch, black hat shading his eyes. Tied on behind the wagon was a cow, and coming from the rear was a girl on a spotted horse. She was herding several loose horses, one of them hobbling along with a badly swollen front leg.

"I'll bet he's a horse trader, don't you?" Jeff said. But Serilda didn't answer. She was watching the girl who was about her own age. Riding astride, her blue, wrinkled dress tucked around her legs, a boy's cap on her brown hair, sleeves pushed up, she wheeled and turned the horse so expertly, Serilda felt a sudden admiration. When the girl rode close, Serilda smiled at her. The girl, in quick surprise, smiled back.

It's as if we knew each other, Serilda thought with a warm, happy feeling. All the way home she kept thinking about the girl, remembering the smile.

Though the day had been warm, the night was

It's as if we knew each other, Serilda thought

chilly. After the supper dishes were washed and candles lighted, the family gathered in front of the big, wide fireplace. Serilda sat on the braided rug, leaned back against her father's knee, and looked around the circle. There was Grandma with her knitting, Ma with her mending, Jeff sprawled in front of the fire, little Bill sound asleep in his cradle, and Pa, so big and strong, behind her. It was good to be here and not down by the river in a covered wagon. The girl had smiled, but there had been a lonely look, too.

"Amos said the new teacher was here. Name is Alexander Moss," Pa spoke up. "He's from the East, and boarding with the Sullivans the first two weeks. School begins at Red Oaks Monday for a five months' term." Pa reached down and stroked Serilda's brown braids. "Reckon you'll have to go alone for awhile, Serilda. As long as good weather holds, Jeff and I will be hauling every day."

"Mr. Ambrose said he would be through with the falsework and start using the big timbers next week," Jeff said. "That will be a sight to see when they push those cords across the river. I sure don't want to miss that. Pa, I don't have to haul or go to school when they do that, do I?"

"It will take more than a day, Son. If you're to build bridges, you've got to learn to figger. Ambrose told you that."

Jeff sighed. Serilda giggled. "You don't have to know much to ride a horse," she said.

"Just the horse," Grandma said dryly. Serilda laughed with the others, remembering the time when the Dentons' horse pitched her over its head.

Later, after Pa had read from the Bible and the fire was banked with ashes for the night, Serilda stretched out on her feather bed and thought happily of the days ahead.

Ma said she might wear her Sunday dress the first day of school and, with it, the gold locket and chain Aunt Matilda had sent her from Boston. She wondered if the girl down by the river had ever gone to a first day of school wearing a pretty blue dress and a golden locket on a fine chain. She wondered, too, if the red-faced man had done anything for the poor, lame horse.

CHAPTER 3

Serilda Makes a Trade

SERILDA SHIVERED with excitement as she hurried into her Sunday clothes. She held her breath as she slipped the blue calico over her head and then gave a long, quivering sigh. She fumbled with the row of tiny buttons down the front. Her fingers seemed to be all thumbs this Monday morning. It would be awful to be late the very first day of school.

"Stop prancin' around, Serilda," Ma said as she took a velvet box from the bureau drawer. She put the fine chain around Serilda's neck. "Here, let me fasten the locket. You have plenty of time."

"But I want to walk with the Dentons, and they go early. And I have the books and the dinner pail both to carry. Ma, I'll really miss Jeff. I wouldn't mind going alone so much if I had a horse to ride. I wish every day for Coaly."

"Pa'll get another horse as soon as he's able," Ma said firmly, "and Jeff will be going with you part of the time. After the first day it won't seem lonely. Here, don't forget your bonnet."

Serilda frowned as she put on the little starched

bonnet. "I feel just as if I had on a bridle," she said as she tied the strings under her chin with a jerk.

Ma smiled patiently and gave Serilda a kiss. "You may feel harnessed up, but you look real pretty. Now be careful of your dress and the locket, and, Serilda, don't play on the way home or stop at the bridge. Come straight home!"

"And remember to learn a little, too, even if it is the first day of school," Grandma added.

There was a crispness in the air that made the little shawl feel good around Serilda's shoulders. She hurried down the hill. The men were already working on the bridge. The movers were still there. The thin woman was washing clothes in a tub, a steaming black pot hung over the campfire. Clothes hung on a line stretched between two trees. One of the little boys was bringing sticks for the fire and the man was sitting on a stump working on a piece of harness. But the girl was not in sight.

The lame sorrel horse with the white stockings was standing under a tree, head hanging down, the swollen leg worse than ever. Serilda felt an ache in her throat. Why didn't the man do something for the horse? If she had a horse, she would surely take care of it.

A moment later, around the curve, Serilda saw the girl sitting on a log, reading a book. She was holding a long leather thong fastened in the bridle of the spotted horse; the other horses were grazing in a little clearing behind her.

Serilda felt the same quick liking for the girl sweep over her. She waited until she was almost even with her, then she stopped. "Good morning," she said. "My name is Serilda Shaw and I live at the top of the hill. What's your name?"

The plain, tanned face lighted up as the girl smiled at Serilda. "I'm Katie Briggs," she said in a soft, slow voice.

"Are you going someplace—or just travelin'?" Serilda asked.

"Well, Paw says we're going south, where it's not so cold. Maw's kinda puny since the last baby came." Katie's blue eyes were troubled for a moment; then she smiled wistfully at Serilda. "You're goin' to school, aren't you?"

"Yes, it's the first day. My brother Jeff goes, too, but he's helping haul lumber for the new bridge now." Serilda looked in surprise at the book in Katie's lap. "That's a fifth reader. Can you read in that?"

"Just tolerable. Maw's teachin' me. She's smart—smart enough to be a schoolteacher. But Paw—his name is Sam Wilson and he is my steppaw; my real one died when I was little—he can't read or write and he doesn't believe in book learnin'. We have six books though," Katie said proudly. "Maw traded her trinkets for them. We have a Bible, a dictionary, a speller, an arithmetic, this reader, and part of a geography. Someday I'm going to live in a real house and go to school." There was a fierce, determined look in Katie's blue eyes. "That's why I do sums and learn words while I'm ridin' along and watchin' the horses Paw swaps for. I'm not always going to be a mover."

"Oh, Katie, you won't have to be. If you keep studying, you can be a schoolteacher—or just anything you want to be," Serilda said earnestly. "I know you can." They looked deep into each other's eyes, almost as if it were a promise.

They talked some more and suddenly Serilda gasped. "Oh, Katie, I forgot. I'll be late for school and have to stay in at recess. Maybe tonight I'll see you." Serilda went running up the hill, the book satchel bumping against her side and the dinner pail swinging back and forth. But the Dentons had already gone.

Serilda made it with only minutes to spare. The schoolyard was full of boys playing ball and dare-base. Inside, a strange man was standing by the teacher's desk. Dressed in a black suit and a white ruffled shirt and black tie, he looked as fine as the preacher. Serilda made a little bow as she passed, feeling suddenly shy in front of this tall, gray-eyed teacher. He looked as young as some of the boys in the yard, but there was a sternness about his jaw and a set to his shoulders that let you know he was older. Serilda put her dinner pail on the shelf with the others. The girls were already sitting on their side of the room in seats they had chosen, the little ones at the front.

Lucy Denton called for Serilda to come and sit with her and Serilda felt proud, for Lucy was two years older.

The schoolhouse was new, built only last year, to replace the old log house. There were rows of double desks and extra benches along the sides of the room. There were windows on both sides and smooth black-painted boards across the front wall where classes wrote their lessons. In the center of the room was a big drum stove that was always red-hot in winter.

Mr. Moss rang the bell and the boys came crowding in, scuffling their feet and laughing. He rapped sharply on his desk, and the room quieted. Picking up a Bible from his desk, he read several verses in a firm clear voice; then he gave a short prayer, asking for guidance through the day. Serilda began to like him right away.

Then, beginning with the smallest girl on the front seat, he asked each one his name and age, writing it down in a record book—the Dentons, Rutherfords, Bradfords, Cannings, Shaws, Sullivans—until all twenty-eight were listed. Jeff would make twenty-nine and there might be more when some older boys finished corn gathering.

Later, when Mr. Moss called for all who could read in the Fifth Reader to come forward, Serilda was glad for her pretty dress and the locket.

"Today you may read until you make a mistake," Mr. Moss said. He nodded to Earl Canning to begin. Earl was so embarrassed he only read one line before he blundered. Some of the others giggled. Serilda waited her turn. Reading was where she shone, and she read the rest of the lesson without a mistake.

"Very good. Very good," Mr. Moss said approvingly. Serilda tried not to look smug. But later, when she missed seven times nine and Earl Canning rattled off the whole multiplication table, Serilda felt her face flush as he grinned at her triumphantly.

The afternoon seemed long. Serilda wished she were up on the high rock looking at her special map instead of the one in the geography. She worked the next day's sums and Lucy whispered they were all correct. She wrote her spelling several times. She wondered if Katie had a slate to use for sums and spelling. She wished that Katie lived somewhere close and they could come to school together and be friends.

After school she walked with Lucy, but she didn't

mention Katie. That was a secret she did not want to share. When she was alone, she ran, her bonnet hanging on her shoulders, the empty dinner pail swinging.

Katie was waiting by the log, her blue eyes anxious and her face unsmiling. "Come set a while and tell me all about school."

"Ma told me not to stop, to come straight home," Serilda said. "But you walk a piece with me and I'll talk fast."

"We mustn't walk that way." Katie looked toward the camp. "There's bad goings-on. You'll have to wait a spell." She hesitated a second, and then she turned to Serilda, her eyes full of angry fear. "Paw's goin' to shoot the lame horse. I just can't stand to see him do it. Maw's got the boys in the wagon."

Serilda stared at Katie in horror, a cold chill creeping over her. "But why—why, Katie—would he kill the horse?"

"Because he says she's goin' to die anyway and he'll put her out of her misery and sell her hide." Katie's eyes filled with hatred. "It's because he's too lazy and good-for-nothin'. He thought he out-smarted the other fellow, getting her for a song, but she was hurt was the reason. Paw said she'd get well. Wouldn't let me take care of her. Thinks he knows everything. Made her walk and walk and walk." Katie wiped her eyes angrily on her sleeve.

"Now she won't eat and the leg gets worse every day. And she's the gentlest, nicest, best horse we've ever had!"

Serilda could not stand it. Anger swept over her. "I know I could cure her," she said fiercely. Then she whirled and went running toward the camp.

"No! No!" she heard Katie shout, but she kept running frantically, her heart pounding, bonnet flying out behind her, dinner pail banging.

She saw the man walking toward the horse with his rifle, and she screamed so loudly that he spun around and stared at her.

"Well," he grunted, "what's itchin' you, screamin' out like a panther?"

"The horse," Serilda gasped. "Don't shoot her! Don't! Give her to me!"

The man's face got even redder. "Missy, I don't give nobody nothin'—not even a dead horse. I can get six bits fer the hide, or swap and mebbe get more'n that. You got six bits?"

"Oh, no, no. I . . . don't have any money." Serilda felt weak. The man looked disgusted, then his eyes suddenly lighted as he saw the chain and locket around Serilda's neck. He almost smiled. "Hmmmm, but you got a little trinket there on that chain. How about swappin' that?"

Serilda's hand flew up to the little gold heart. "But I can't swap that! I can't."

[25]

He shrugged and turned toward the horse.

Serilda clutched the little gold locket and stared at the horse. Head hanging, feet spread apart, hair dull and rough over the bony frame—she was the sorriest-looking horse Serilda had ever seen. Then the horse moaned a little, holding the swollen leg up, as if asking for help.

Serilda snatched the chain and locket from her neck. "I'll swap! I'll swap!" she cried. "Don't shoot her, please don't. And I'll make her live, too." With shaking fingers she dropped the locket in the man's outstretched hand.

For an instant he looked surprised; then he dropped the locket in his pocket, laid his gun on a stump, and went over to the horse. Untying the old halter he handed it to Serilda. "There, missy, she's yours, hide and all; and I'll throw in the halter for good measure. You've got yourself a horse."

She stood for a minute, trying to think. Then she reached out a trembling hand and patted the white spot in the horse's forehead. She spoke softly, and the horse turned her head a little and opened her eyes. A sudden, deep determination filled Serilda's heart. She leaned close. "You're my horse now," she whispered, "and you're going to get well. Do you hear me? Now, come, let's go home." She pulled gently on the rope. The man spoke sharply and gave

[26]

the horse a slap on the rump, and she took a stumbling step.

Out in the road Katie was waiting, a smile on her tear-stained face. "Her name is Star," she said softly, "and I believe you can make her well." And her look was so thankful and loving Serilda knew they would be friends forever.

So a step at a time Serilda and Star started up the long steep hill.

CHAPTER 4

The Long, Dark Night

SERILDA WAS glad that the men who were working on the bridge had gone home and that Amos Carter was not on the ferry. Never had the hill looked so long and so steep.

She tugged on the halter and the horse took a crippling step; then they rested, then they took another step. It seemed they hardly moved at all. Serilda choked back the tears and petted and talked and pulled again on the halter.

Halfway up the hill was a spring by the side of the road. Here, Serilda took her dinner pail and brought back water. She patted the thin, trembling body, and her hand was trembling, too. "Oh, Star, don't give up! Don't stop! Some day we'll ride like the wind."

It was then she heard Jeff calling and saw him coming down the road with Grover.

"Where've you been? Ma's worried half to death and Pa's mad." Jeff stopped stone-still, his chin sagging. "Serilda, what you doin' with the mover's old crowbait?"

"She's not crowbait. She's a horse. And she's mine. I swapped for her. Oh, Jeff, he was going to kill her," Serilda burst out sobbing.

"Swapped for her? What . . . what did you swap?" Jeff asked in astonishment.

Serilda could hardly say the words. "My . . . my locket."

Jeff stared unbelieving. "You mean your gold locket . . . and chain . . . that Aunt Matilda sent you?"

"But it was all I had, and he was going to shoot—right that minute. Jeff, please don't look at me like that." Serilda choked back a sob. "I had to do something, and do it quick. And she's a good horse; she just needs . . . loving and taking care of. I'd rather have a horse than a locket anyway."

Jeff stood silent. Grover sniffed around the strange horse and stood waiting.

Finally Jeff took a deep breath. He walked around the horse, and then he leaned over and looked at the swollen leg. Serilda looked at Star and her heart ached.

Then Jeff straightened up, and the frightened, accusing look was gone from his eyes.

"You pull, Serilda, and I'll push; whatever you do, don't let her lie down. If she ever does, we'll never get her up again."

It was almost dark when they got to the top of

the hill and turned into the dooryard. Pa was waiting at the gate.

"Serilda, where have you been since school was out?"

Serilda took a long breath. "I've been—helping my horse up the hill," she stammered chokingly. "Oh, Pa . . . I . . ."

"Your horse! Serilda, what have you done?"

Serilda felt an awful sinking in her stomach and she put her hand on the horse's neck. Jeff stood beside her, and Grover licked her hand. Then she told her father the whole story.

Serilda had never seen Pa so angry. His voice was cold and sharp when he spoke.

"Serilda, you've disobeyed your mother. You've ruined your Sunday clothes. You've traded off a gold locket for a dying bag of bones. That man is a schemer, and he took advantage of you. And I'm going down and tell him so. I'll get the locket and he can come and get the horse."

"Will?" Ma's voice came from the steps where she was listening. "Supper is ready and waiting. Come and eat. Then we can decide. In the dark is no time to argue with a stranger."

Pa stood for a minute before he turned toward the house. His face was flushed and he seemed like a stranger himself. Serilda wondered achingly if she would ever again see the twinkle in his eyes.

Jeff helped Serilda get the horse to the back yard and tied to a tree. Then they went to the house. Ma looked at the dirty blue dress that had been so fresh and clean that morning; then she looked at Serilda's neck where she had fastened the locket. There was a look in her eyes that hurt more than words. All she said was, "Change your dress, Daughter. Put on the old gray linsey."

Supper was eaten in silence; only little Bill had anything to say. Serilda could hardly choke down the corn pone and baked potatoes. Even the hot gingerbread and honey stuck in her throat.

Pa, too, ate little. He shoved his chair back from the table and looked across at his daughter, his glance stern. "Serilda, your mother is right. It's best to wait till morning to straighten this out. Then we'll return the horse and get the locket. But while the horse is here we'll do what we can to keep it alive. Be as bad as the mover if we let it suffer."

Serilda went out into the darkness, Jeff beside her. One night's care wouldn't make Star well. The mover would shoot her after all. Please, God, she prayed in her thoughts, help us to make her well.

Pa came out, carrying coals on a shovel. "Get some kindlin' and we'll build a fire under Ma's wash-pot and heat some water. Then we'll get the old iron kettle and soak her foot and leg in hot salt water. Just like Ma did for you, Jeff, when you ran that big splinter in your foot. We'll do what we can."

Soon the salt water was ready and the horse, too sick to care, let them put her foot in the kettle. As the water cooled, Serilda added more hot water. The horse stood quietly, head down, eyes half closed. Pa offered her water but she would not drink; and she paid no attention to corn held under her muzzle.

Serilda tried to swallow the hard lump in her throat. Even if the mover got the horse, she wished with all her might for it to live.

"That's all we can do," Pa said after awhile.

"Pa, can't Jeff and I stay up tonight and take turns watching?" Serilda begged. "Keeping the water hot might help a lot."

Pa looked at the horse and then at Serilda. Finally he nodded his head and turned toward the house.

In awhile Grandma came out, a pan in one hand, a long-necked quart bottle in the other. She looked at the horse and shook her head. She squinted into the kettle at its foot and leg. Then she turned to Serilda, her eyes a little sad.

"If she's going to get well, she has to have something in her stomach to go on. Too sick to eat. I've mixed up some eggs and honey with milk. It's real strengthenin'. Jeff, throw that halter rope over a limb and pull her head up. Serilda, you steady her." Before the horse knew what was happening, Grandma pushed the neck of the bottle in the side of her mouth and poured the reviving mixture down her throat.

She ran her wrinkled hand down the side of the horse's neck and over her ribs. "She feels plumb cold. You better get that old comfort out of the shed to put over her." They stood quietly looking at Star. Then Grandma handed Serilda the pan. "There's more here you can give her later, if you think she needs it." She sighed and turned toward the house.

It was late when Ma came out, bringing a thick comfort and an old quilt. There were two pieces of gingerbread, too. She looked at the horse, wrapped in the old comfort, with its foot in the kettle. Then she looked at the children, and Serilda had never seen Ma so sad.

"One of you had better rest while the other one watches," Ma said as she spread the comfort on the ground. "Remember, there's timbers to haul tomorrow and another day of school."

She bent to kiss Serilda. Suddenly Serilda was sobbing, with Ma's arms tight around her. "I'm sorry, Ma . . . about not coming straight home . . . and about the locket. But I had to help Star. I couldn't let her be killed. And the girl, Katie . . . she couldn't stand it either. Ma, I've wanted a horse. I've missed Coaly so."

"I know," Ma said quietly and she patted Serilda's shoulder. "Pa knows you miss Coaly, but he needed the big team for hauling more than you needed Coaly. He'll get another horse as soon as he can." Ma stood quietly for a minute, then she went back to the house.

Serilda and Jeff sat down on the comfort and talked. Back in the woods a hoot owl called and over toward the Dentons', a wolf howled. Later, they managed to give Star the second quart of the mixture. Then Jeff built up the fire, filled the wash-pot with water, curled up on the comfort, and went sound asleep. A pale sliver of moon shone dimly in a starless sky, but the firelight made a warm circle in the darkness around the horse and the two tired children.

All the worry and the trouble of the evening settled in Serilda's heart. She put her hand against Star's neck and the tears streamed down her cheeks. The horse turned its head and gave a weak little nicker.

It seemed hours later when Grover growled suddenly and looked toward the road. Serilda put her hand tight in his thick hair and hushed him. She thought she heard a horse. A twig snapped, and then all was still. A shiver of fear ran over her.

Then Katie stepped softly out of the shadows and motioned to Serilda, a finger on her lips.

"As soon as you took the horse," Katie whispered, "Paw decided we'd leave early this morning. He made us get ready. I slipped off to tell you good-by.

I could see the light from your fire. He thinks I'm getting the horses. Look, Serilda, I wanted you to know." She pulled the gold locket from the neck of her dress. "Maw got Paw to give this to her and she gave it to me for a keepsake. Serilda, I'll wear it and remember you always."

Serilda threw her arms around Katie and gave her a quick squeeze. "Oh, Katie, I love you, and I'll remember, too."

"And listen," Katie whispered tensely, "don't tell anyone I've been here. I think Paw's got something that by rights is yours." A horse's footsteps sounded in the road. "That's my horse. I've got to go. Good-by, good-by."

Serilda stood listening, until the last soft footfall of the horse died away. Jeff slept on, unaware of the visitor, but Grover walked back and forth beyond the fire, eying the darkness.

Serilda built up the fire and warmed the salt water. She put her hand underneath the old comfort. Star felt warm. "Thank you, God," she whispered; then she sat down near the horse's head and leaned back against the tree. Grover stretched out, head on paws, beside her. It was a long night. What would Pa do now? And what did Katie mean when she said, "Paw has something that by rights is yours?"

Serilda awoke with a start. Someone was shaking her. She felt cold and afraid.

"It's Pa, Serilda. You and Jeff get up and go

into the house and get in your beds. I'll take a turn with the horse." His voice was tender and loving. Serilda flung her arms around his neck and buried her face on his shoulder. "Oh, Pa, I'm glad you've come. I'm sorry—I traded off the locket—but I had to save the horse—"

Pa held her close and stroked her hair. "But, Daughter," he said huskily, "you have to mind Ma and me. When you make a promise, you must keep it. When you want to swap for something—ask us."

Serilda rubbed her face against Pa's shirt.

"I've been thinking tonight," Pa went on. "We'll leave things be as they are. You've lost the locket, and you may lose the horse, but you made your own decision. Ma and I think it's best for you to abide by it."

A great peace settled over Serilda.

"Pa," she asked shakily, "if I keep Star, can I stay home and take care of her? Maybe that will make her live."

"Yes, tomorrow," Pa agreed. "You'd be no good at school after tonight. Now, it's late. Wake Jeff and go to the house."

"Pa, I'll learn every word in that old speller. I really, truly will," Serilda said gratefully. And Pa smiled with the old twinkle in his eyes.

CHAPTER 5

Good News

BREAKFAST WAS a gay meal. Serilda spread butter on a pile of corncakes and topped them off with comb honey. Never had fried hominy tasted so good. Even the mug of milk seemed sweeter, for Star was better. She had swallowed two more quarts of Grandma's mixture. She had drunk some water, and she opened her eyes wide when her name was called.

Serilda thought of Katie's secret visit and wondered how far the movers had gone. And what was the mysterious thing Katie's pa had that belonged to Serilda? Could it be a bridle that belonged to Star? Or a saddle? She was glad the man had gone, but she wished Katie could have stayed. She and Katie could have gone to school together, instead of Katie's studying all by herself along the roadside.

Later, when Pa and Jeff had gone to the mill and the sun was bright, Serilda took the comfort from Star's back and, with currycomb and brush, cleaned the rough hair and combed the tangled mane and tail. When she had finished, she hurried to the house to get Ma and Grandma.

"Doesn't she look better? Isn't she clean and slicked up?" Serilda rubbed the scrawny neck and patted the bony shoulders. "Ma, when she gets fat and shiny, she'll be the color of your amber sugar bowl. Kinda gold, under the brown. She'll be beautiful."

Ma smiled and walked around the horse. "She looks better than she did last night. I'll say that much. But she'll never get fat and shiny unless she eats. Why don't you mix up some cornmeal mash and tempt her with that?"

"Let's take a look at the leg," Grandma said. "Maybe it has soaked long enough." She bent over and gently touched the swollen leg. "It's had enough salt water," she said. "We'll spread some of the herb salve on a cloth and wrap around the leg. That's mighty healing."

Grandma straightened up and looked at Serilda, her brown eyes twinkling like Pa's. "You know, she might turn out to be a high-stepper like Colonel Thompson's thoroughbred. There's just no telling."

Ma laughed and gave Serilda a squeeze. Serilda's heart sang. A high-stepper like Colonel Thompson's thoroughbred! If Star could only look like that!

Serilda was so busy all day taking care of Star and studying her lessons that she could hardly believe it when she heard the squeak of wagons. It was Jeff and Pa and she ran out to meet them.

"How's Star?" Pa asked at once.

"She drank a lot and ate a little. And Grandma thinks she might turn out to be a high-stepper like Colonel Thompson's thoroughbred," Serilda bragged.

Jeff grinned and Pa smiled, too. "Sounds like your horse is better. How'd you like to put her in Coaly's stall? Have to take care of these thoroughbreds." He chuckled. "Got your lessons for tomorrow?"

"Almost." Serilda slipped her hand into Pa's big strong one as he walked along beside the oxen. "I will get them, every single one, even that old arithmetic."

Pa was pleased. "That's a promise," he said as they turned into the driveway.

In the morning Star was standing, but she had lain down during the night, for there was straw clinging to her flank. She began to eat the warm mash at once. Serilda laughed with joy as she patted the thin shoulder.

"You're better, and you can stay right here and get well. Today I have to go to school, but tonight I'll be back again." She put hay in the manger and left a bucket of water in the corner of the stall. Everything was fine.

Pa and Jeff left for more timbers soon after breakfast. It was cooler this morning. Gray clouds scurried overhead and the first hint of winter was in the air.

Serilda wore a linsey-woolsey dress and a brown wool jacket, and she tied a red crocheted fascinator over her braids. It seemed more than a day since she had been to school, so much had happened.

The men were working at the bridge, but the camp site was deserted. The log where Katie had sat was empty, too. Serilda swallowed a lump in her throat. She wished, with a strange loneliness, for Katie to be here with her, laughing and talking on the way to school.

Lucy Denton was waiting at the top of the hill, and she wanted to know why Serilda had been absent from school.

Serilda dreaded to tell her, for Lucy would spread the news. Serilda could see the boys laughing and the girls staring in unbelief. They'd think she was plumb silly to trade her locket to a mover for a sick horse. But Star wouldn't always be lame; sometime, when she rode her to school, high-stepping and shining, they'd wish she belonged to them. Serilda took a deep breath and with quick determination told Lucy all about it.

Lucy stared at Serilda as she listened to the story. "But Star is going to get well and be the finest horse in the whole county," Serilda finished triumphantly.

Lucy looked dubious and shook her head. "Maybe you're right, but that sure was a pretty locket. I'd think quite a spell before I'd give it up for an old crippled horse. That mover was just too slick for you. Pa says you can't trust a horse trader as far as you'd throw a bear by the tail." Lucy shrugged. "But I guess if you'd rather have a bunged-up old nag than a gold locket, I should mind. Everybody to his own likin'." She shrugged again and began talking about all the things the new teacher had planned—literary society every other Friday night and singing school the Fridays in between, and spelling and ciphering matches. "But he sure expects us to have our lessons—and no fooling around." Star seemed to be forgotten.

Serilda took Lucy's advice and did not fool around, but her thoughts wandered away to the thin lame horse with four white feet, and she lost her place at the head of the spelling class. She would have to do better than this if she were going to learn all the words in the speller. She was glad when the day ended.

It was a week later when she was hurrying home that she heard a shout from the bridge. She stared in amazement as a familiar figure walked along the falsework toward her. It was Jeff, grinning all over his face.

"What are you doing up there?" Serilda demanded.

"Watchin' 'em lay the cords. They're halfway across on the north side." He pointed to the big square timbers, stretching out like a path across the scaffolding. "You ought to see how they do it. Halve the ends back two feet, lay 'em together, bore holes, and peg 'em fast. Sounds easy, but it's lots of work."

"But how did they get these heavy things out there without horses?" Serilda looked puzzled.

"Well, you don't have to have horses for everything," Jeff snorted. "They put wooden rollers, like Ma's rolling pin, under 'em. It's like two solid timbers reachin' clean across the river."

Serilda looked at Jeff and marveled at how smart he was.

"And when they get the braces in the sides and the top cord on, they'll put long rods from top to bottom and tighten 'em until they actually lift the bottom cords off the falsework," Jeff explained importantly. "They'll lift it until it is arched in the middle—that far." He measured the length of his hand.

"Come on, let's go home." Serilda laughed. "You've seen enough."

They raced up the hill and ran breathlessly into the kitchen, where Ma was lifting a kettle of apple dumplings from the fire. Serilda sniffed eagerly, and Jeff smacked his lips and peered into the kettle. Then he began telling Ma and Grandma all about the bridge.

Serilda slipped a long-sleeved apron over her dress and stuck an apple in her pocket and ran to the barn.

Star nickered softly as Serilda went into the stall beside her. She lipped the pieces of apple from Serilda's hand and plainly asked for more.

Star was improving every day. The big bays, a little uppity at first, finally accepted her, and Grover began sleeping in her stall at night. Serilda brushed, combed, fed, and watered her, and sometimes Pa and Jeff gave a hand. A layer of fat began covering the bony frame and the dull hair began to shine. In a few weeks the leg was completely healed, leaving only a long red scar. The halting limp disappeared.

Several times Serilda took short rides after school, riding slowly and easily up in the pasture, exercising Star's tender muscles. One day she went to meet Pa and Jeff as they came from the mill. Star was so prancy Pa said he thought going to school would be good for her. This was the news Serilda had been waiting for.

Up early the next morning, she hurried to the barn. While Pa and Jeff milked, she brushed and combed Star, put on the folded blanket, and belted it down tight with the surcingle. It was much more fun to ride bareback with just a blanket than tucked up on a sidesaddle. A measure of oats in Coaly's old feed sack and Star was ready to go.

Serilda felt as prancy as Star. She fairly flew into her dress, the brown jacket, fascinator, and warm mittens. Ma had made a long sack that held the dinner pail and books in one end and the feed sack in the other. Serilda put it across Star's shoulders, slipped onto her back from the stile block, tucked her skirts around her knees, and was off. She waved to Ma and Grandma, who were watching from the doorway.

Star knew this was a special day. She snorted little clouds of breath into the crisp December air. And when a rabbit jumped out ahead of her and skedaddled down the road, she shied like a colt.

Prickles of excitement ran over Serilda. This was her horse, taking her to school—her very, very own horse! They went sedately down the hill and passed the bridge at a walk; then they cantered by the campgrounds and Katie's log. There Serilda loosened the reins, and Star took the slope at an eager gallop. It was as easy as Grandma's rocking chair. If only Katie could see her!

At school everyone in the yard gathered around when Serilda rode in and tied Star to the hitching rack.

"Is that the mover's horse? Is her leg all right?" They wanted to know everything. Star looked wise and rubbed her nose on Serilda's shoulder, and Serilda gladly answered every question. Such a horse for a locket! The boys looked at Serilda with admiration, but the girls were not so sure. They talked until the bell rang.

It was a clear morning, but by afternoon the sun was hidden by gray clouds. When school closed at four o'clock, it had begun to snow and there was a sharp wind from the north.

Star pranced and danced, and one of the boys held her until Serilda could get on. Then Star settled into a long easy lope that took them home in a hurry.

Pa was at the barn when Serilda rode in. He looked at Star and gave her a pat. "Nothing wrong with this horse. She's fit as a fiddle." He looked at Serilda and his eyes were teasing. "I'll bet if that mover ever comes this way again and sees how fine she looks, he'll try to claim her."

Serilda laughed at Pa's joke, but the thought came back to haunt her time after time.

CHAPTER 6

The Bridge Is Saved

THE STORM that began the day Star first took Serilda
to school turned into a blizzard that whipped across
the hills and filled the valleys deep with drifts. It
was the first of many snows that did not melt all winter long. Grandma said it was the coldest, stormiest
winter she could remember.

Frost glistened between the logs on the inside
walls of houses. Quail, wild turkeys, and prairie
chickens came to the barnyard to eat with the tame
geese and chickens. Wolves, gaunt and fierce, killed
some of the Dentons' sheep.

Work on the bridge was at a standstill for weeks.
The floor was on, braces in, the top cords and some
of the rods placed; but the bridge still rested on the
falsework. The ferry froze solid in the river and the
few travelers crossed on the ice.

The school term ended in February, and Serilda
felt as if she and Jeff had hardly gone at all, there
had been so many stormy days.

Through the long, bitter winter, Serilda thought
of Katie. Had her pa really meant it when he said
he was going south, or were they huddled around a

campfire with only the wagon for a windbreak? Was Katie wearing the locket? And what was it Katie's pa had that Katie wanted to give her? Serilda thought about it over and over. But more than anything she wished Katie could see Star. Maybe in the spring they would come this way again.

But it seemed that spring would never come. Snows lay on the ground through March and into April, but finally warm rains began falling, melting the snow and turning the creeks into raging torrents. Ice in the river began breaking up, and huge cakes of ice floated like rafts in the muddy water. Amos Carter tied up his ferry, and went for a visit with his daughter at Spring Hill.

Then came a week of sunshine that poured over the drenched and frozen hills. Dandelions popped out, scattering their gold along the roadside, and purple violets lifted dainty faces to the sun.

On Sunday Pa said he was going to cut across the pasture and visit a neighbor. Jeff and Serilda decided it was a fine time to hitch Star to the buggy and go down to the river.

Star, loose in the barnyard with Tib and Tony, threw up her head and let out a shrill whinny when she heard the familiar whistle. She trotted to the gate, her little pointed ears cocked forward and her eyes shining as Serilda and Jeff came toward her.

Star could hardly wait to get started. She pawed

impatiently and tugged on the lines. Ma waved from the steps and Jeff waved back, but Serilda was too happy to do anything but drive. She turned Star toward the river. A tingling joy seemed to fill her whole body. Star felt it, too.

The air was clean and clear. Across the valley, hills were sharp against the sky. A haze of new green hung over the treetops. It was a good day.

As they went down the hill, Jeff looked ahead intently. "Say, the river's lots higher than yesterday. I can see brush and stuff coming down the river. And the ferry's swinging crazylike. Serilda, something's wrong. Let's get a move on."

Serilda shook the lines and clucked to Star. The buggy lurched and the mud flew. In a moment they were by the river. Jeff was out of the buggy, running, before they stopped. Serilda tied Star to a tree and ran to stand by Jeff.

The muddy water churned and boiled as the current came swiftly around the bend. It caught the ferry, shoving it against the bank, then jerking it out again into the swift water, swinging it back and forth like a huge pendulum.

"Rope's broke at the far end. Nothin' holdin' the ferry but that one rope." Jeff pointed to where a smaller rope was tied to a tree behind them. It was stretched taut as a fiddle string. "If the ferry breaks loose, it'll smash the bridge," Jeff yelled, and he ran toward the ferry. Serilda screamed, but Jeff ran on. As the ferry swung in, he jumped over the rail, ran to the other end, and pulled out the broken rope. As he dragged it back, Serilda ran to the edge of the water and yelled for him to throw the rope to her.

As the ferry swung back and touched the bank, Jeff flung the rope over the side. Serilda grabbed and held on. With a leap Jeff hit the ground beside her. Panting and struggling, they pulled the heavy rope toward the nearest tree. It was too short to reach.

"The lines—I'll get the lines from Star's harness," Serilda panted.

"Not stout enough. Get Star—loosen the singletree from the buggy. We'll tie to that. Hurry!"

Serilda flew to the buggy, loosened the clevis, and hurried Star back to Jeff. He looped the rope around the singletree and tied it fast.

The ferry swung out and the rope tightened. Star laid back her ears and strained forward, her eyes wide with shock. She pulled with all her strength. Halfway out, the ferry slowed.

"She stopped it!" Jeff shouted. "She's pulling it back to the bank!"

It was true. Leaning against the harness, her sharp hoofs digging into the soft earth, Star was slowly dragging the ferry back against the current.

[49]

"But she can't last!" Serilda cried. "She'll hurt her leg! Get the hay rope. It'll reach the tree. Run!"

Jeff whirled and started running with all his might for the long, thick rope they used at haying time.

Star stood braced, holding, straining. Serilda leaned close, stroking her neck. "You're my fine horse. Keep the rope tight. It's for the bridge, Jeff's bridge, our bridge." She said the words over and over, hoping, praying, talking, trying to give Star strength.

And Star held steady, leaning against the pull with all her might. Sweat poured down her heaving sides, muscles quivered. But gradually the proud head drooped and her breath came in short hard gasps.

Words were ragged sounds as Serilda stared at Star and then at the empty road. It seemed hours since Jeff had gone.

Then she cried with relief. Jeff was in sight, running down the hill. A few minutes more and Star would be free.

She turned to Star and the river. A huge log with cakes of ice jammed against it was coming round the bend. Serilda stood, rigid with fear, as the log came nearer and nearer. It hit with a grinding crash, and Star, lunging frantically against the sudden load, was dragged to her knees.

She struggled, wild-eyed, groaning, gasping. But slowly, surely, she was being pulled backward to-

ward the River. Serilda cried out! She hated the river
—the ferry—the bridge! She'd get Star loose. The
bridge could go!

She grabbed at the tugs and jerked and pulled
with all her might. Taut with strain, the tugs held
fast! Tangled in harness and rope, Star would drown
in the river. Desperately, Serilda grabbed the halter
rope and flung herself on the ground in front of
Star, digging in her heels, helping her pull. She
shut her eyes tight and gave a strangled prayer:
"Dear God, help us quick!"

Suddenly Jeff was there. He pushed the end of
the hay rope through the loop of the other rope,
ran to the big tree, went around it twice, and tied
the knot. The ferry was anchored fast!

Serilda scrambled to her feet. Together, Serilda
and Jeff loosened the tugs. Star was free! She stag-
gered up and stood before them, quivering, the lovely
white legs and silken tail caked with mud and sweat.
Serilda threw her arms around Star's neck. "Oh,
Star, you're safe! You're safe! The river didn't get
you!" She squatted beside Star and felt of her knees,
rubbing the scarred leg. Star was not hurt. She was
all right! Serilda sank back on the ground and sobbed
a thankful prayer.

Jeff, too tired to talk, leaned limply against the
tree. The bridge was saved.

Suddenly there was a shout. Pa was calling and

running toward them. "What's happened? Somebody hurt? I was in the pasture and I saw Jeff running with the rope. Thought someone was in the river."

When they told him what had happened, Pa's face lighted up and his dark eyes shone. He looked at the unfinished bridge over the flooded river, at the ferry tied snug against the bank, and at the mud-caked children and the exhausted horse.

He put his arms around Serilda and Jeff and held them close. "Steve Ambrose is going to be mighty thankful for this—and Amos—and everybody in the county," Pa said huskily, his voice warm and tender.

Then he rubbed Star's nose proudly and picked up her halter. "Come on; let's go home and tell Ma and Grandma. They'll be as glad as I am."

In a few days the river was back to normal, and Star was rested. The struggle at the ferry seemed like a bad dream.

Busy days stretched into weeks. Serilda helped Ma with the weaving, house cleaning, soapmaking, hoeing in the garden, and all the spring work. It seemed there was never time enough to sit on the high flat rock or ride a shining sorrel horse.

Pa and Jeff were busy, too, working late in the fields when they were not hauling for the bridge. But the hauling was almost over. Men were putting up rafters for the roof and, when that was done and the sides boxed in, the bridge would be finished.

Underneath, most of the falsework was still standing, but long ago the rods had been tightened and the bridge lifted until it arched in the center.

It had been a busy time and, when word was passed around that a new family up by Spring Hill was having a barn-raising, it was a cause for celebration and everyone planned to go; even the men working on the bridge said they would lay off for the day and give their services.

Serilda began counting the days, for going to a barn-raising was almost as much fun as going to the county fair.

CHAPTER 7

Jeff Has an Accident

IT WAS THE day of the barn-raising and barely sun-up. The Shaw family, up long before daylight, was almost ready to go. Pa, standing by the side of the wagon, looked up at Ma and little Bill on the spring seat, then at Grandma snug in her chair behind them. He leaned over the side of the wagon and began checking.

"The basket of vittles, hammer and saw, the plane and adz, and feed for the horses. Guess we have everything." He turned to Jeff and Serilda, his dark eyes understanding.

"It does beat all that Old Shortie had to pick the day of the barn-raisin' to have her calf. But every man will be needed to lift the heavy logs and get 'em placed before dark, and the women folks will have to do a lot of cookin' to feed 'em. If we didn't go to help, the Randolphs would have a mind to think we were unneighborly. You're a heap more help stayin' home today."

"Serilda, you rid up the house. There's fresh smearcase, and soup to warm and molasses pie in the cupboard," Ma said. "And, Jeff, remember to split some kindlin'. We'll be home by dark." Ma smiled reassuringly. "And if there's any cake I'll bring you some."

Grandma smiled, too. "Something nice will come along to take the place of the barn-raising. Always does," she said comfortingly.

Pa clucked to the big bays and they started. Little Bill, puzzled that Serilda and Jeff didn't go with them, waved until they were out of sight down the hill.

Serilda looked at Jeff and brushed at the tears in her eyes. "Everybody and his cousin will be there but us and we're stuck at home because Old Shortie is so contrary. Wants to have her calves way out in the woods somewhere instead of on the bed of nice clean straw Pa fixed for her. Other cows don't act that way!" Serilda kicked angrily at a rock.

"Other cows aren't Old Shortie," Jeff said. "She's got a mind of her own. And beside that, she's the best cow we have, and Pa doesn't want to take any chances losing the calf. Last year Pa and I hunted two days before we found her and the calf hid out in a thicket. If it hadn't been for Grover, guess we never would have found her. Had to carry the calf the last half a mile it got so tuckered out. And we got tuckered, too."

They listened as Old Shortie bawled and butted the barn door.

"I'll go and talk to her and maybe that'll help," Jeff said and turned toward the barn, Grover tagging along behind.

Serilda looked up in the pasture where Star was grazing by the big flat rock and some of her resentment melted away. Maybe she couldn't go to the barn-raising, but she had a horse—the prettiest, fastest one in the whole world! She'd hurry and wash the dishes and straighten up the house and, maybe if Old Shortie hurried, too, there would be time this afternoon to take Star and go somewhere.

But Old Shortie took her own good time and it was after three o'clock in the afternoon before she had a little brown heifer and nearly four before it was on its wobbly legs and getting its first dinner. It was too late to hitch up Star and go anywhere for a drive before chores, but there was still time to go up in the pasture and eat apples and look at the map and visit with Star.

It was then that Jeff remembered the kindling. "It won't take but a minute. I'll do it while you're getting the apples," he said as he hurried to the chopping block and picked up the ax.

Serilda ran to the cave for a handful of apples, then into the house for slices of bread spread thick with butter. She wondered how long it would be before the folks came home. It had been a long day.

Suddenly the chopping stopped and a terrifying scream split the air.

"Serilda! Seril . . ."

Serilda flew out of the door. Jeff was crouched by the chopping block, squeezing his bare right foot tight in his hands. He looked up at Serilda, his eyes wide with fright. "The ax hit a knot and slipped and cut my foot, bad, awful bad! What'll we do? Everybody's gone!"

Cold fear clutched Serilda's throat. Not a neighbor for miles around that hadn't gone to the barn-raising. Even Amos had taken off for a few hours. She tried to think what Ma or Pa or Grandma would do if they were here.

"I'll get some water and clean cloths and we'll tie it up, tight. That'll make it stop." She ran to the house and back again. But when Jeff released the pressure of his hands, the cut spread wide and ugly and the blood ran down his foot. He grabbed it tight again.

Serilda gasped, then she ripped off a strip of cloth and tied it tight around Jeff's ankle and the bleeding slowed, but Jeff's leg began to ache and turn blue and they had to loosen the cloth.

Serilda looked at Jeff's white face. She must not let him know how scared she was. Her thoughts raced. There was a doctor at Chillicothe, the closest place, but she'd never been to town without Pa. But Pa wasn't here. She knew, suddenly, what she must do.

"Listen, Jeff," she said, squatting beside him, "I'm

going to hitch Star to the buggy and take you to the doctor. Lie down and prop your foot up on the chopping block so it won't bleed so fast and don't be scared. We'll make it all right. Star will get us there." Serilda tried to keep her voice from shaking. She straightened up and gave a shrill whistle and Star, out in the pasture, answered with a high, glad whinny and came trotting to the pasture gate.

Serilda ran for the harness and, almost before Star was through the gate, had the bridle on her head and the harness on her back. She whispered to Star as she fastened the tugs and buckled the lines together. "Star, you have to go faster than you've ever gone before. Jeff's cut his foot bad and he's bleedin' somethin' awful. You have to take us to the doctor!"

Star perked her ears and pawed impatiently. She was ready.

Serilda ran to the house and got a stool and a pillow and some more cloths. Grabbed up a slate and wrote: *Jeff cut foot and gone to doctor in Chillicothe.* She braced the stool against the dashboard, laid the pillow on it, and turned to Jeff. She put more cloths around his foot and tied the string tighter around his leg. "We'll loosen it when we get in the buggy," she said as she worked fast. "Now hold to me."

With Serilda pushing, Jeff got into the buggy, his foot propped up on the stool, the pillow underneath.

[58]

Serilda looked at Jeff's drawn face and her heart almost stopped. Already there was a red spot oozing through the thick cloths and they were over three miles from the doctor. Would they ever make it in time? What if the doctor weren't there?

Serilda jumped in the buggy beside Jeff and picked up the lines and spoke to Star. "We're going to make it all right," she said to Jeff. "Now, you hang on!"

Star, eager to go, stepped out at a swinging trot. Serilda knew she must not push her too hard at first. At the end of the first mile Star began to slow. Serilda urged her on and Star went back to the swift steady trot. Then it was two miles and the sweat ran dark on Star's sides. For just a minute Serilda let her walk a few steps as she loosened the string around Jeff's ankle. Not once had they met anyone.

"The spot! Serilda, it's getting bigger!" Jeff cried out in terror and keeled over into Serilda's lap. Serilda looked. The spot was getting bigger!

Her heart jumped to her throat. She gave Star a quick, sharp cut with the lines. "Go! Star! Go!" she yelled. Star plunged forward, running, her ears laid back and her white legs reaching out. Flecks of foam flew back from her heaving sides and the buggy swung from side to side on the rutty road. Serilda braced herself on the footrest, holding on to

Jeff with one hand, the lines with the other. "Help us to get there, God. Help us to get there." Serilda said the words over and over as the wind whipped her face and stung her eyes.

Far down the road she saw a horseback rider and a team and wagon. The rider turned out to let them pass. It was Colonel Thompson on the big black stallion. "The doctor!" Serilda shouted as they went by.

There was an answering shout and suddenly the big black stallion was running ahead, clearing the road for them. "Make way! Make way!" Serilda heard the Colonel shout when he met the team and wagon. The startled driver made way.

As they reached the edge of town, Star began to slow, weaving a little, her breath a rattling gasp for air.

"Star, you've got to go on! You've got to go!" Serilda cried chokingly and struck Star again with the lines.

And Star, summoning her last bit of strength from deep within, ran behind Black Chief clear to the doctor's door!

Colonel Thompson sprang from his horse and lifted Jeff out of the buggy and carried him into the doctor's office.

"He cut his foot," Serilda said shakily as they laid him on the table and the doctor began to take

The stallion was running ahead, clearing the road for them

off the cloths. "Ma and Pa were gone to the barn-raising and all the neighbors, too. I brought him to you as fast as Star could come." Serilda faltered and looked at the doctor. "Are we in time?" she whispered.

The doctor felt of Jeff's pulse, looked at the cut, then he smiled at Serilda. "A whiff of chloroform and a few stitches and he'll be good as new in a week or two."

Jeff opened his eyes and looked at Serilda. "Don't leave me," he said weakly and reached his hand toward her.

"I won't leave you," Serilda promised and stood close beside him, holding his hand tightly.

The Colonel gave Serilda a pat on the back. "While you and Doc are patching up your brother, I'll take care of your horse."

The doctor got a strange-looking tin cone, stuffed in a wad of cotton, poured on a few drops of a pungent, clear liquid, and held it over Jeff's nose. Soon Jeff went limp. Then the doctor pulled up a chair. "Sit down," he said to Serilda and handed her the cone. "I need your help. When he begins to stir, hold the cone over his nose again. Try not to breathe it yourself. It won't take long. Now you watch him, not me."

Serilda took the cone with shaking fingers and sank into the chair, staring at Jeff's white face. Twice she had to put the cone over Jeff's nose. And all the while the choking tightness in her throat got worse. She thought of all the fun she and Jeff had together . . . how smart he was, the finest brother anyone could ever have . . . better than bridges, horses . . . anything. She fought to keep the tears back. She mustn't fail Jeff now. She prayed silently.

Suddenly the doctor reached over and took the cone from her hand. "We're all through. You're a fine assistant! There was a small artery cut and he could have bled to death. You're a brave little lady, and your brother owes his life to you."

Serilda leaned her head against the table and tears of relief filled her eyes. "It wasn't me that saved him. It was Star," she said brokenly. "She brought him here, but I had to whip her."

"She'll forgive you." The doctor chuckled. "I'll watch your brother while you go out and get a breath of fresh air and see about your horse. The Colonel might need some help."

But Colonel Thompson didn't need any help. He had unhitched Star and put a blanket over her back and was walking her slowly up and down the street. She pricked up her ears and whinnied when she saw Serilda and Serilda felt her heart almost burst with pride.

"Fine horse you have here," the Colonel said. "Not many could come as far and as fast as she did. That last quarter mile showed what kind of horse she is, for she ran it with her heart, after her strength and breath were all gone. She just kept on going because you asked her to." He smiled and held out his hand to Serilda. "I want to shake hands with a brave little lady. Lots of grown folks wouldn't have had the quick wits to do what you did. I'd say you and your horse are a couple of thoroughbreds."

Serilda felt her face flush as she took his hand. "But you cleared the way at the last and made it easier," she said gratefully.

"When she cools off some more, we'll give her a drink of water. Doc through with your brother?"

"Yes, and he's going to be all right. My, but I'm glad," Serilda said, a great load slipping from her shoulders.

Later, when Jeff was awake, the doctor carried him out to the buggy and propped his foot up on the stool. Jeff leaned his head weakly against Serilda and managed a smile.

"Stay off your foot until next week, then come in and we will take out the stitches. Serilda, drive carefully and don't shake him up too much." The doctor smiled at them encouragingly.

Serilda picked up the lines, dreading the trip home. It would be dark before they got there. She wished with all her might for Pa and Ma.

Colonel Thompson stepped over and began untying the big black. "I'll ride along behind you so I can help if you need me," he said.

"Oh, I'll be so obliged if you will." Serilda gave a deep breath of relief and spoke to Star.

They passed Colonel Thompson's house at the edge of town and then halfway home dark overtook them, Jeff, dozing half asleep, Colonel Thompson keeping pace behind them. It seemed a week since morning.

Far down the road Serilda heard the creak of a wagon and Star suddenly threw up her head and gave a neigh of welcome. Tib and Tony answered. It was Pa and Ma coming to meet them.

Serilda tried to explain everything, as Colonel Thompson and Pa lifted Jeff up and put him on a pallet in the back of the wagon. Ma put her arm tight around Serilda as she listened, then she leaned over and kissed her. "You're the finest daughter anyone could ever want," Ma said in a strange husky voice that didn't sound like her at all. Then she climbed up in the back of the wagon and sat down beside Jeff.

Star was tied to the endgate to follow with the empty buggy. The Colonel was thanked and he said good-by and rode away.

Serilda climbed up to sit on the spring seat by Pa. In the darkness he turned to her, his voice warm and tender. "Daughter, if you get to be the wife of a president of the United States, I couldn't be any prouder of you than I am right now. You saved your brother's life by your quick thinkin'." He gave her a hug that took her breath. Then he picked up the lines. "And I sure thank the Lord for the day you dragged Star up the hill. She's earned her keep forever."

Serilda leaned happily against Pa and a warm, drowsy feeling slipped over her. Suddenly she sat up straight. "Pa," she said, "I forgot to tell you. Old Shortie had a heifer!"

CHAPTER 8

Visitors

IT WAS A week later when Serilda, busy washing the dinner dishes, heard hoofbeats. She hurried to the window in time to see Colonel Thompson on Black Chief ride into the drive.

"It's Colonel Thompson," she said in a shrill whisper over her shoulder, "and he's coming in!"

Ma got up from the loom and smoothed back her hair and took off her apron and Grandma laid aside her knitting. Jeff sat up on the edge of his cot, a delighted grin on his face.

Serilda went to the door and watched as Colonel Thompson tied Black Chief to the hitching post. He was a tall man, ramrod straight, with thick gray hair and a gray mustache. His skin was ruddy, his smile warm, and his gray eyes friendly. He came across the yard with long swinging strides and took off his wide-brimmed hat when he saw Serilda and her mother at the door.

"Had a little message to deliver and thought I'd stop and see how Jeff was getting along and if he was on his feet yet. Doc said that was a pretty mean cut."

[67]

"Come in and set awhile. We're real glad to have you. Jeff's doing fine. Will made him a crutch, and he's been hobbling around a bit. Tomorrow he goes in to have the stitches out. Serilda, take the Colonel's hat."

"And how are you, Miss Serilda?"

"I'm fine, thank you," Serilda said.

"And the little mare?"

"She's fine, too." Serilda straightened with pride as she took the Colonel's hat and hung it on a peg.

The Colonel shook hands with Grandma and they sat down by Jeff and began to visit. They had talked only a little while when Serilda caught the faint, shrill whinny of Star out in the pasture. Then came a sudden loud, answering neigh from Black Chief. Serilda slipped out of the door as Star came running down from the pasture into the barn lot, her head flung high, prancing and curving and tossing her mane like a filly. No longer the sweat-stained, exhausted mare that Black Chief had guided to the doctor's office, but shining and alert she thrust her head over the gate toward the admiring stallion.

He pawed the ground and his eyes flashed as he arched his neck and gave another bugle of welcome, trying to reach the gate where Star was waiting. He snorted and twisted, pulling on the reins, his whinny loud, demanding, then suddenly turning to soft little whickers that Star answered with soft little whickers of her own.

Serilda stood transfixed, her heart pounding with pride and fear as the black stallion got more excited, wheeling and curving his shining body, straining to free himself from the hateful reins. She tried to call the Colonel, but no sound came.

In the barn lot Star danced and pranced, her feet barely touching the ground, her mane floating and rippling as she paraded before Black Chief. Never had she seemed so beautiful to Serilda and never had Black Chief been more awesome, his muscles shimmering like prairie grass in the wind. His nostrils wide, dark eyes fiery, his black tail a plumed banner.

Serilda felt as if she were swept up in a strange wild dream. Suddenly, as she watched, Black Chief gave a powerful backward pull that broke the reins and jerked the bridle from his head! He was free! Serilda screamed as he reared upward and gave a ringing challenge. Then he ran to the gate and charged against it! There was a thudding crash, but the boards held. For an instant he stood there, his head close against Star's. Then he ran back down the drive, whirled and flashed toward the gate, crouching for a second as he gathered his legs for a spring that carried him flying over the gate into the barn lot!

Behind her Serilda heard Colonel Thompson yell as he came tearing across the yard, but it was too late. Black Chief flung out a ringing bugle to Star and raced toward the pasture, where he circled and whinnied, demanding her to follow.

As if spurning the ground, Star raced to Black Chief, and side by side the two running horses seemed to float out of sight over the hill, their heads together, tails rippling in the sunlight, the stirrups of Black Chief's saddle swinging empty in the wind.

Colonel Thompson ran to the hitching post and grabbed up the broken bridle, his face white with chagrin. "Old and rotten! I should have known better!" He dropped it with disgust. He stared at the hill where the horses had vanished, then he turned to Serilda. "Quick! Get me a rope I can use for a lasso."

"No! No! Colonel Thompson, you'll be killed! The Chief is wild! He jumped the gate!"

"He's not wild, he's just excited," the Colonel said.

Ma hurried out. "Colonel Thompson, don't try to catch him by yourself. Let Serilda run and tell Will. He's cultivating corn in the south field, right next to the pasture. Grover is with him and he'll help, too."

Colonel Thompson frowned and hesitated for a moment. "That might be better. Serilda, please get me the rope and I'll go myself and tell your father.

If we can't catch him, we'll drive them back here and get them into the barn. The stallion is not vicious, Mrs. Shaw, so don't worry."

Serilda brought the rope and the Colonel hurried out of the yard, leaving the broken bridle lying on the ground. She shivered with fear and excitement as she looked out toward the hill where the horses had disappeared.

The sheep were resting under a tree in the corner of the pasture. Old Shortie and the other cows were grazing peacefully over by the big rock. High overhead a hawk curved and dipped in widening circles against the clear blue sky. Even the chickens and ducks and geese, that had scattered so madly from Black Chief's flying feet a few minutes ago, were again scratching contentedly in the barnyard.

But Serilda's heart was beating as wildly as ever. She caught her breath in a quick little gasp and leaned over to pick up the broken bridle from the ground.

"Take the bridle to the shed, Serilda," Ma said worriedly. "Maybe Pa can mend it for the Colonel."

Finally, the Colonel and Pa returned leading Black Chief, Star walking along beside him, Grover trotting out in front.

Serilda, watching, held her breath as Pa opened the barn door, but Star went docilely into her own stall. Then Black Chief went in behind her and was guided into Tony's stall where the Colonel tied him to the manger. There he stamped and pawed in the strange stall, raising his head high to look over the partition at Star.

Later, when Pa had mended the bridle and Colonel Thompson was ready to leave, he suddenly reached in his pocket and took out a square white envelope, an embarrassed smile on his face.

"In all the excitement, I almost forgot to deliver the message that the county court entrusted to me. It is a bit rumpled now, but the contents are un-harmed.

"It gives me great pleasure," he said with a smile and a little bow as he handed the envelope to Serilda. Then he mounted Black Chief and rode away.

Serilda turned the envelope over wonderingly. It was addressed to Jeff and Serilda Shaw and sealed impressively with wax. She opened it with trembling fingers, Jeff leaning on his crutches, the others watching. She took out the stiff, folded paper and spread it flat.

"*To Jeff and Serilda Shaw,*" she read in a hushed voice.

> "*In appreciation of services rendered during the spring flood, at which time, without thought of your own safety or that of your gallant horse,*

you courageously worked to save the new bridge.
"WE, the members of the LIVINGSTON
COUNTY COURT, STATE OF MIS-
SOURI, do hereby extend to you and your gal-
lant horse, Star, the honor of leading the parade
and being the first to drive across the new cov-
ered bridge on opening day, August 1, 1867."

To lead the parade with Star! Serilda tingled with
amazement. She looked around the circle and then
back at the letter in her hand. Suddenly she ran
toward the barn. "I'm going to show it to Star," she
yelled back over her shoulder.

She held the invitation up in front of Star's face
and solemnly read it through. Star pricked her ears
and listened. Then she looked past Serilda into the
empty stall where Black Chief had been and gave
a little nicker.

"He's gone," Serilda said, "but we're here! Oh,
Star, I've so much to think about I can hardly stand
it." She laced her fingers through Star's mane and
leaned against her. "I wish," she said with a wistful
sigh, "that Katie knew all about today."

Ma said the parade called for a new dress and
bonnet for Serilda and copper-toed boots for Jeff,
even if he could wear only one.

Grandma said she would make red yarn tassels
for Star's bridle and the big bays, too. Pa said he

[73]

would tighten the buggy and give it a new coat of paint.

"Serilda," Pa said, half serious and half joking, "you'd better not let anything happen to Star. She's the most important horse in the county right now."

A sharp fear ran over Serilda. After the last few days, what more could happen to Star?

CHAPTER 9

The Bridge Opening

SUCH A HURRY and flurry! Before anyone could believe it, the bridge opening was only two days away. And right in the middle of things, when Ma was sewing the buttons on Serilda's new dress, little Bill poked three of them through a crack in the floor.

"Serilda, you'll have to get on Star and ride over to the Dentons'. Lucy's mother bought some buttons like these the same day I did. Maybe she has extras. Don't stay."

Serilda put on a fresh dress, tied on her sunbonnet, and skipped to the barn. It was too bad little Bill lost the buttons, but it would surely be good to have a ride.

At the foot of the hill a new road branched off to go across the bridge. Approaches were filled in and wooden bannisters had been built along the sides. The clutter of lumber and rocks had been cleared away; even the falsework was gone. A temporary fence was stretched across the bridge until opening day. Firm and solid on the rock abutments, the bridge reached across the river like a long, empty house, waiting for visitors.

Suddenly, to Serilda, it was more than a bridge; it was a friend, ready and waiting to help through all the years ahead. There was awe in Serilda's heart at the thought of the years. Would the covered bridge still be here when she was old like Grandma? When people rode across, would they ever think of all the men who worked to build the bridge? Would they wonder who hauled the stone and timber?

She reached out and smoothed Star's sleek neck, a new feeling in her heart. "Star, when we cross the bridge," she said softly, "we must go proudly. It is an honor, not just for Sunday, but for always."

Across the river the white blur of a moving wagon came toward the ferry. Serilda's heart quickened with the sight of every covered wagon, hoping it might bring Katie.

There was much talk at the Dentons', but soon Serilda started home, the extra buttons pinned in her pocket. She would have to hurry.

As she rounded the curve by Katie's log, a covered wagon was pulling into the little clearing. A woman was driving, and a girl about Serilda's age was sitting hunched over on the seat beside her. Behind came a heavy-set man, riding on a gray horse and herding several others. Star threw up her head and neighed at the strangers.

Serilda went closer; the girl on the front seat looked

familiar, but thinner than Katie. Suddenly she caught her breath. It was the movers! She reined up by the wagon as it stopped and Katie straightened up and smiled.

"Katie! Katie!" Serilda shouted. "I've watched every wagon. I've hoped and hoped you'd come this way again. Katie, are you sick?"

Katie nodded.

"She's been puny ever since we camped by a swampy place last spring. I think it's the ague. She gets to feeling right spry and then she starts having chills and fever again," Katie's mother said worriedly. "Paw said she ought to wear it out by this time, but I think she needs some quinine."

Katie had been only half listening as she looked at Serilda and then at Star, her eyes wide with amazement.

"Serilda, I want to know. Is that really Star?"

Serilda nodded proudly and patted Star's neck.

"I can't believe it," Katie said. "She's the prettiest, slickest horse I've ever seen. Ah, Serilda, I'm so glad you have her." She smiled then and pulled the locket from the neck of her dress where Serilda could see it.

"Say," a gruff voice said close beside them, "let's take a look at that horse you got for nothin'. Been feedin' her up a mite, ain't you?" He looked Star over and then reached down and ran his hand along the scarred leg. Star tossed her head and stamped uneasily.

Fear ran over Serilda and she nudged Star to move away, but the man grabbed the bridle. "Not so fast, missy. Not so fast." He looked up at Serilda, his eyes sharp as steel. "I got a right to look at this horse. You think that old brass chain paid for her? Well, it didn't. She's mine, and I can prove it. Katie, give the gal back her brass trinket. I'll take my horse."

"Your horse!" Serilda burst out angrily. "We traded fair and square. You can't have her. Take your hands off that bridle!" She tried to jerk the bridle loose, but the man held on, twisting the bit cruelly in Star's mouth. Stung with pain, Star pulled back, her sharp hoof coming down on the man's foot. He swore and dropped the bridle. Serilda stuck her heels in Star's flanks and with a snort Star plunged and began running.

Serilda heard the man yell, but it was lost in the rush of wind and flying hoofs. Trees went by in a dizzy blur and Serilda clung with all her might to Star's thick mane. Up the hill Star sailed. She stopped so quickly at the barnyard gate, she almost pitched Serilda over her head.

Serilda cried out as she slid to the ground and dragged open the gate. Pa, Ma, and Jeff came running.

"The mover—he's come back. He tried to take

Star!" Serilda said brokenly. "He said he could prove she was his. Oh, Pa, he can't take Star away from me, can he?"

Pa put his arm around Serilda and held her tightly. "Tell me exactly what happened." Serilda told him. Pa's jaws set hard and his brown eyes grew cold and stern as he listened.

"That man needs to be taught right from wrong! I should have done it before." Pa gave his hat a yank and started toward the road, but Ma grabbed his arm. "Will, listen to reason. Don't go down there, getting yourself into a mess. Get folks all stirred up and the parade only two days off. No telling what would happen. Wait until after the parade, then teach him, if needs be."

"But what if he comes to get her before the parade?" Serilda cried.

"He'll not get her," Pa said grimly. "And after this parade is over, we'll settle it. Don't you worry, Serilda. We'll keep Star in the barn at night and Grover will tell us if anything goes wrong."

"I saw Katie, too. She's sick with chills and fever. Had it ever since spring. Her pa was riding herd and she was sitting all hunched over on the seat by her mother."

Serilda tried not to be afraid, but the words, "I can prove she's mine," kept coming back again and again. How could he prove it when Katie had the locket?

[79]

That was proof he got paid. If only she could talk with Katie. But Katie was not the same; thin and yellow, her eyes heavy and dull, she looked as if she were too tired to care.

It was a quiet night. The next day Ma and Grandma cooked for the basket dinner. Pa and Jeff washed the wagon and polished the harness. Serilda combed and brushed Star until she glistened. She washed her white legs with Ma's soft soap and polished her hoofs with beeswax. Pa said she looked like a show horse. Serilda's pride was mixed with worry. The prettier Star looked, the more the mover would want her.

The next morning was bright and clear. Serilda gave Star one final polish, and everything was ready.

In the house she turned and primped before the looking glass on Grandma's bureau. Wearing her new blue challis dress, pantalets with lace-edged ruffles, straw bonnet lined with pink challis, black lace mitts, and black gaiters with gray tops, Serilda had never felt so stylish.

Jeff, too, looked spruce in his gray linsey-woolsey pants and a fine white shirt, with ruffles like Pa's Sunday best. A new straw hat sat on his slicked-down hair and on his feet were the new copper-toed boots that he wore without a limp. Serilda and Jeff looked at each other admiringly.

The old buggy, too, looked fine, with a shiny black body and bright red wheels.

Long before time for the parade, people were

going by in wagons, buggies, and carts, and afoot and on horseback. Serilda was shaking with excitement as she got into the buggy.

"Serilda, watch your driving through the crowd," Pa cautioned. "And if Star balks about going through the bridge, you get out and lead her, Jeff. And don't worry about the mover. He wouldn't do anything in a crowd."

Serilda clucked to Star and they were off.

"People—I never saw so many people. Hundreds of 'em on each side of the river," Serilda said, amazed. "It's like town on Saturday. And there are horses everywhere."

Star knew she was on parade. She bowed her neck and arched her silken tail and stepped so high and handsome that everyone turned to look.

"There's Mr. Ambrose standing at the bridge— and the judge and the preacher." Jeff squirmed in excitement. "Say, everybody's here! They have a white ribbon stretched across the opening of the bridge. Look! There's Colonel Thompson on Black Chief and he is clearing a path for us. You s'pose the Chief will act up again?"

"What'll I do if he does?" Serilda tightened the lines, a worried frown on her face. "I never thought about that."

But Black Chief had his mind on helping the Colonel get the parade in shape.

Serilda searched the crowd to see if the movers

were there. Then she saw Katie and her mother with the boys, standing in a little group by themselves. The man was not in sight. She smiled and waved at Katie, and Katie waved back. She looked so thin and wistful, it made Serilda's heart ache. If it hadn't been for Katie's caring, there would be no shining, proud-stepping Star. Suddenly Serilda pushed the lines into Jeff's hands and said, "I'll be back in a minute."

She hurried through the crowd, straight to Katie. "Come ride with us over the bridge," she said. "I want you." She looked up at Katie's mother. "She can come, can't she?"

Katie stared in astonishment, but her mother's face was radiant. "Of course, she can ride with you."

"Oh, Serilda," Katie whispered as they went back to the buggy, "Paw'll be awful mad, but I never was so happy."

They got into the buggy, Serilda in the middle, Jeff and Katie on either side. Out across the crowd, Serilda spied Katie's pa, glaring at them, his face red and angry. She pretended not to notice.

They listened to speeches about the bridge. Then the judge stood up and smiled. "To Jeff and Serilda Shaw, their friend Katie Briggs, and their beloved horse, Star, we give the honor of being first to cross the new bridge." He clipped the ribbon and made a bow, and the crowd cheered.

Without a quiver, Star walked proudly up the

They had crossed the bridge

approach and onto the covered bridge. There was time for only an excited word or two. Then another ribbon was clipped, and they were out into the sunshine again. They had crossed the bridge! They pulled to one side to watch as others followed through. Then they went back to the camping grounds for the big basket dinner.

Later that evening, when chores were done and candles lighted, a knock sounded on the door. Serilda caught her breath and looked at Pa. Had the mover come after Star?

Pa opened the door. It was Katie's mother.

The woman's face was white and drawn, and her dark eyes troubled.

"I am Nellie Wilson, Katie's mother," she said as Pa asked her in and she sat down in a chair. "I feel as if I know you, Katie has talked so much about Serilda. I was so proud when you asked Katie to ride with you across the bridge, everybody looking so fine and Star stepping so high. It was an honor." She smiled at Serilda. Then she hesitated and took a deep breath.

"I'm troubled. I've come to ask a mighty big favor. First, I want to apologize for the way Sam scared Serilda about taking Star away from her. He was just mad when he saw what a fine horse he let get away. He is a queer man. When he traded for Star, he said she was a thoroughbred, but he wouldn't take care of her. He had a paper that he locked up in his little tin box. I never read it. He carries the key on a leather thong around his neck. But I actually don't put too much store by papers he gets, for he can't read or write and he's been fooled by folks time and again. I guess it doesn't make any difference since she is just a pet of Serilda's."

"But she might have a foal by a thoroughbred sire. That would make a difference," Pa spoke up.

Serilda looked intently at Pa and then turned earnestly to Katie's mother. "Oh, Mrs. Wilson, is there any way you could possibly see the paper and know for sure?"

"No, not now. Sam is put out about Star and he is stubborn as a hickory stump. But if I ever get a chance I'll look at the papers and, if one of them is Star's, I'll send it to you."

Mrs. Wilson sat quietly for a minute before she spoke again. "We are on our way to the Far West. Sam says he is going to join up with a wagon train in Westport that is starting for the Oregon country in three weeks. We are leaving in the morning. He has quite a bunch of horses he is going to swap for vittles and gear to take us on the journey. The train plans are to make it to Fort Laramie and winter there.

"It is a long, long way and there're Indians and mighty high mountains, but he has promised to settle down and homestead a place when we get there. I'll look forward to that."

She worked her hands nervously in her lap and Serilda felt a terrible lonesomeness in her heart, knowing she would never see Katie again. Why did they have to go clear to Oregon to homestead when there was land to be had in Missouri?

"The favor I'm asking is"—the woman swallowed hard as if the words choked her—"can Katie stay here and live with you folks? She has been puny with the ague, off and on, ever since spring and Sam won't do nothing for her. Treats her just like his horses. If they get sick, they either get well or die. No coddling. He is good to his own boys, but he has always resented Katie and given her the hard row to hoe. I don't know whether it is because he likes boys best or because she is not his.

"But I've done all I know to do. If she had rest and some medicine, she'd get well. But he won't buy it and I haven't any money. I'm just afraid she won't ever make it to Oregon . . . and there never was a finer girl." The woman's voice broke and Serilda felt her own eyes fill with tears.

Then the woman straightened her shoulders. She looked at Ma and Pa. "It's asking a lot to take in a perfect stranger, but Katie will more than earn her

[86]

keep when she gets well. If I ever get to Oregon and settled down, someday, I'll make some money and send it to you."

Pa cleared his throat and started to speak, but the woman was not finished.

"Before you answer—I want so much for Katie to go to school. She hankers for it and learns quick. But that means books to buy and it takes money. I want you to think of that, too." She waited, her hands twisted in her lap.

There was a long look between Pa and Ma and the room was quiet except for the squeak of the cradle as Grandma rocked little Bill to sleep. Jeff shifted uneasily in his chair and Serilda could hardly breathe as she waited for Pa to answer. To have Katie here everyday like a sister! To share all the fun and work together!

Pa looked gravely at Mrs. Wilson. "What if Katie didn't get any better? What if something would happen?"

Mrs. Wilson smiled. "I heard folks talk at the bridge opening today, saying how fine a family you were, one of the first settlers, honest and hard-working and kind. And there is a feeling in this room of peace and love and a look on your faces that makes a good home. Katie would get well here, I've no fear of that!"

Pa smiled back at Mrs. Wilson, then he looked

again at Ma before he spoke. "We'll take your daughter, Mrs. Wilson, and treat her as if she was our own. So set your mind at rest," Pa said gently.

Serilda jumped up and threw her arms around Pa's neck and ran and kissed Ma, too, and, for good measure, Mrs. Wilson!

Suddenly the tears were streaming down Mrs. Wilson's cheeks as she put her arm around Serilda.

"I must go now and tell Katie. We will put her things in a bundle and stop by in the morning as we start on our journey."

She turned at the door, her face radiant.

"May the Lord bless all of you, now and for always," she said softly as she left the circle of light and walked away into the darkness.

CHAPTER 10

Plans for the County Fair

IT WAS THE last of September and nearly two months since Katie had come to live with them. She was almost well again. Her cheeks were getting round and pink, her blue eyes shone, and her happy laugh mingled often with Serilda's.

It was a busy time, with kraut to make from the late fall cabbage, apples to pick and dry, pumpkins and squash to bring in from the cornfield and store in the cave.

Pa and Jeff had been busy building a new shed for the sheep. Ma and Grandma had threaded the loom for a hit and miss rag carpet, and Katie and Serilda had tacked rags for the carpet and wound them into balls until Serilda said she knew there was enough to reach around the world! Candles had been made, too, for the long winter evenings, and wool from the spring shearing carded and spun into yarn. Even the wild hops had been gathered for Grandma to make into yeast.

But tasks were fun with Katie to share them. Washing the sticky mush pot and scouring the steel knives and forks with ashes went in a hurry when there were exciting things to talk about. And there was much to talk about.

Work had started on a new gristmill down by the bridge, with the walls of the forebay half finished. Then the second week in October school was to begin. But most exciting of all was the county fair that would be the first week in October, three days of it, and all the family planned to go for at least a day.

Pa brought home a printed premium list from the county seat. "Seems even better than last year. Reckon there is a prize for 'most everything. Brass band's going to play and all kinds of entertainment." He laid the list on the table.

The children crowded around.

"Ma, listen," Serilda said. "For best coverlid, first prize, one kerosene parlor lamp! Ma, did you hear that?"

"Look, here's a prize for the best draft team," Jeff read excitedly. "Pa, you can take Tib and Tony. Nothin' can beat 'em. And first place is ten dollars! And here it says, 'Best single driving horse, shown by owner.' Serilda, look at that. That's ten dollars, too! And best riding horse! First, ten dollars—"

"Ten dollars," Serilda said faintly, "for best driving horse?"

"And ten dollars for best riding horse. You can enter, too. Serilda you'll be rich!" Katie said.

"Pa, oh, Pa, can I take Star to the fair and drive her? Can I?" Serilda held her breath.

Pa smiled and nodded his head, but Ma frowned.

"Will, do you think it would look seemly for a girl to be driving in a contest with grown men? What if some horse got cantankerous? I think it is dangerous, and people might criticize us for letting Serilda ride and drive. I've never seen a girl or woman drive or ride in a contest, have you?"

"No, can't say that I have," Pa said smoothly. "But I don't know of any girl in the county that owns a horse as fine as Star. Maybe that's why we've never seen one."

Ma turned to Grandma. "What do you think about it? Should Serilda ride Star at the fair, before the public, competing with men? Do you think that is ladylike?"

Grandma looked up from her knitting. She was thoughtful for a moment. "Pretty is as pretty does," she quoted. "If Serilda minds her driving and acts like a little lady, I think there would be no criticism."

Ma sighed and smiled a bit ruefully at Serilda.

Serilda ran to Grandma and gave her a kiss, then she grabbed Katie and spun around the room. "And can Jeff and Katie ride with me in the buggy?" She asked breathlessly.

"It says, shown by owner. That means just you.

Jeff and Katie will have to watch, like the rest of us," Pa said.

"But I can help now," Katie said quickly. "One time we watched people drive at a big fair in Illinois. They drove this-away." She sat up ramrod straight, elbows turned out, imaginary lines held chest-high, eyes straight ahead.

Serilda and Jeff burst out laughing, Katie looked so stiff and strange.

"It's the truth," Katie said earnestly. "They did drive that way. And the horses were trained to walk and trot, but no matter how fast they trotted they mustn't break into a gallop. And when they stopped before the judges, the horses put their front feet even and their back feet even. They arched their tails and bowed their necks and stood still as stone, the best ones. They stood that way even when the judges walked around looking at them. A man who trained 'em told Paw all about it and I heard him."

Pa smiled. "That was way back East, where they put on airs, Katie. The judges won't be that particular here."

"What are you going to do with the money, Serilda?" Jeff looked proudly at his sister.

"She doesn't have it yet," Pa said. "Star won't be the only one. I heard there are quite a few good horses now. The Colonel had a new buggy brought in from Brunswick and a fine set of harness. He will enter Black Chief as a single driver. Last year he got first. And I reckon there is not a better riding horse in the state than the black stallion."

"Pa!" Serilda was shocked. "You know there is one as good."

Pa smiled at Serilda's flushed face. "The judges will decide that, Daughter."

"But a lot of it will depend on how you ride and drive her," Katie said earnestly. "Let's begin practicin' tomorrow."

The next day Serilda and Katie hitched Star to the buggy and drove to a level spot in the pasture. Katie was the judge and took a stand. Serilda sat up straight.

"Drive to the oak tree, turn left, and walk her back," Katie said.

Serilda giggled and Star flicked her ears as they went to the oak tree and came back.

"How was that?" Serilda asked.

"Fair to middlin'!" Katie said. "Now do it again, only turn right and come back on a high trot."

Back and forth Katie sent them and, when she finally signaled for them to stop and Serilda pulled up in front of Katie, Star stood square, neck bowed, tail arched, feet together, ears pricked forward.

"She knows! She knows!" Katie cried jubilantly. "She's done it before, Serilda. She recollects. She's been to fairs!"

Serilda jumped from the buggy and ran to Star's head. She threw her arm around Star's neck and twined her fingers in her thick mane. Star nickered softly, nuzzling Serilda's shoulder. "You're fine as corn silk," Serilda said proudly. "It will take more than Black Chief to beat you."

Serilda practiced riding, too, trying to sit up straight in the sidesaddle while Star walked, trotted, and loped. But the sidesaddle was uncomfortable after being used to riding bareback and astride. And Star wanted to go too fast.

"She has been raced sometime in her life," Katie said after they stopped practicing one day. "As soon as you get in the saddle, she wants to run. She is not that way hitched to the buggy."

"She can go fast hitched to the buggy, too," Serilda said loyally. "And she can hold out. She ran nearly all the way to town when Jeff cut his foot and at the last, when she was almost winded, she kept up with Black Chief, and he was fresh."

"But the judges at the fair won't know all that, Serilda," Katie said with a little sigh. "It's just what you do that very day. You will have to practice more on your riding."

The fair started on Wednesday and all exhibits and entries had to be in by noon. Horses were to be shown and judged on Thursday, beginning at ten

[94]

in the morning. Draft horses in the forenoon, riding and driving horses in the afternoon, and cattle and oxen and hogs the day following. Serilda knew the premium list by heart.

The Dentons were not entering any animals, but planned to take their entries of vegetables and grain in early Wednesday.

They offered to take the Shaws' entries, too.

Tuesday, Pa and Jeff brought in a huge yellow pumpkin, a fine crook-necked squash, ears of yellow field corn, and fat little ears of popcorn, also apples from the orchard, and a head of cabbage from Ma's carefully tended garden. Then Grandma's best quilt and Ma's Sunday-woven blue-and-white coverlid, the "Indiana Rose," were carefully folded and put in clean pillowslips, ready to go.

Wednesday, Ma and Grandma cooked things for their dinner the next day. Serilda and Katie pulled the buggy up in the yard and washed it clean with soap and rainwater. Pa said the water would help take out the rattle, too. Then they rubbed it with beeswax until the red wheels glistened. The harness, too, was waxed, and the red tassels Grandma had made for the bridge opening were fastened to the bridles. Pa and Jeff cleaned the wagon and then all of them brushed and curried and washed the horses until they shone.

"Folks may have bigger pumpkins and better

cabbage," Serilda said wearily as she ate her supper, "but I'll bet nobody has any cleaner horses. Ma, if you get the parlor lamp as the prize for best coverlid, can we light it every night, or do we have to save it for company?"

"If I get it, we'll light it every single night," Ma promised.

CHAPTER II

The Shaws Go to the Fair

EARLY THE next morning the Shaws started for the fair. Pa, handsome and proud, driving the shining bays, with Jeff and little Bill beside him. Grandma and Ma dressed in their Sunday best were sitting in chairs behind them. Following came Serilda driving Star, with Katie beside her. In the wagon were baskets of food, currycomb and brush, rub cloths for the horses, saddle blanket and sidesaddle, and Star's bridle. They had everything.

Serilda had never felt so gay, Star had never been so prancy. Prickles of excitement raced up and down Serilda's spine and she looked at Katie and felt happy clear to her black-and-gray gaiters.

The trees were brilliant with scarlet and yellow, and along the roadside plumy goldenrod and purple asters mingled with the flaming red of sumac and orange bittersweet. A covey of quails ran along the dusty road and then flew with a sudden whir into the meadow. Up in a tall hickory tree a squirrel barked as they drove by. Overhead wild geese, in a wide V winged their way south for the winter. It was a perfect day.

[97]

There were many travelers going to the fair for it was the main day. As they passed through town and turned into the route to the fair grounds, the road grew crowded. Suddenly a man driving a high-stepping dapple gray, with a plumy white mane and tail, cut swiftly around them, leaving the Shaws trailing in a cloud of dust.

"He's not so smart," Serilda choked. "I've got a good horse, too. I could show him."

Katie was silent for a minute. "Serilda, that horse was traveling too fast for this time in the morning. It won't last all day. But it was a good horse and so is Black Chief, and your paw said there would be more good ones. You mustn't lose your temper or you'll be licked. You must do what the judges tell you. If you get rattled, Star will, too."

Serilda stared straight ahead. There just couldn't be a better horse than Star; gray or black, it made no difference.

As they turned in at the gate to the fair ground, they could hear the brass band playing a marching tune, muted by sounds of rumbling wagon wheels, bawling cattle, neighing horses, hawkers crying out their wares, and the soft hum of hundreds of people talking. There were smells, too.

Serilda forgot the gray horse and tilted up her nose and took a deep breath, her eyes shining. "Whiff it, Katie! Don't you just love it?"

Katie took a long, delicious breath. "It's popcorn and cider and lemonade and molasses taffy. And hog meat fryin' and coffee boilin' and wood smoke and sweat and dust and the smell of all the animals, mixed up and floatin' around."

"And you can't tell which is which," Serilda said. "It's just the 'fair smell.'" Serilda and Katie laughed together.

They drove around the edge of the crowd and Pa stopped under a big tree. The draft horses were to be shown this morning, the riding and driving horses after dinner.

"We'll go first thing and sign up and pay the entry fees," Pa said as they tied the team. "Then we'll come back and get everything slicked up." Serilda and Katie followed Pa and Jeff, but Ma and Grandma and little Bill stayed with the wagon.

They followed Pa through the crowd, waving and calling to neighbors, past the brass band playing, the tents of exhibits. A quick stop for a drink of water from the shining new tin cups swinging from the wooden barrels. A sniff of the hot buttered popcorn. A mouth-watering look at the tubs of lemonade. Serilda, tingling with excitement, her hand tight in Katie's, hurried after Pa. After it was all over, they could take their time and see everything, for Pa had given each one a whole dime to spend as they pleased.

They came to the ring, a level place in the pasture, roped off for showing the animals. It was a long oval with a well-worn track around it. In the center of the oval a man sat at the judges' stand, a big tin horn beside him for announcing. A few benches sat beside a table with a sign that said: PAY ENTRY FEE HERE. It was soon over and Pa and Serilda had signed their names. For the first time Serilda felt a quivering in her stomach. It was easy to ride Star bareback to school or out in the pasture, but on a sidesaddle and here before everybody—that was something else. A sudden choking filled her throat.

Back at the wagon, Serilda and Katie slipped long-sleeved aprons over their dresses and, while Pa and Jeff groomed the big bays, they unhitched Star and brushed and rubbed her until she shone like Ma's copper kettle. Then they wiped every speck of dust from her white legs and the star in her forehead and her nostrils and eyes. They dusted the harness and buggy, too.

The Shaw family stood close to the ring as entry time came for the draft horses.

"Here they come. Pa's leadin' the line!" Jeff almost fell over the rope in his excitement. Serilda's heart thumped as Pa drove around the oval, the big, powerful bays stepping solidly together, muscles rip-

"Here they come. Pa's leadin' the line!"

pling, their broad chests pulling against the wagon as if it were a toy. Ma stood up straight and Grandma's eyes were proud.

"The others don't have a chance," Jeff crowed as they watched the different teams put through their paces. As a last requirement each team was hitched to a bobsled, loaded with rocks, and asked to move it.

Horses sweated and strained and fell to their knees, some drivers swore and yelled and used the whip, but only one team moved the sled a few inches. Serilda could hardly bear to look.

Then it was Pa's turn. He hitched Tib and Tony to the sled; checked the harness, gave each a pat as he went by and picked up the lines. He had no whip, but his voice rang out.

"Tib! Tony! Git up an' go! Dig outta here!" And Tib and Tony responded! They leaned over and their hoofs dug into the dry earth and they pulled together! Veins stood out on their necks like whipcord. Powerful muscles grew taut as the sled slowly began to move . . . a foot . . . two feet . . . ten feet . . . twenty feet and Pa hollered, "Whoa! That's enough!"

The crowd cheered and yelled. Serilda felt weak and Jeff leaned against a post. The Shaws took a long breath of relief when the judge handed the blue ribbon to Pa. "First prize and ten dollars in gold for best heavy draft team goes to Will Shaw and his bay Percherons."

Pa took off his hat and smiled and Ma's face grew pink, her eyes twinkly. If I can only do as well, Serilda thought.

The basket dinner was spread on a checkered red cloth, with the blue ribbon right in the middle. Thinking of what was to come, Serilda could hardly eat a bite and Ma and Pa didn't urge her.

Afterward, Jeff gave Star a final polish, while Pa girted on the sidesaddle. Serilda slipped the new, long green riding skirt on over her dress and hooked it securely. Ma tied a green bonnet that matched the skirt over Serilda's braids. She gave her a comforting squeeze. A quick lift from Pa, and Serilda was settled in the saddle.

She took a deep, quivery breath and picked up the reins. She looked down at Katie and suddenly wished they could change places, for Katie was part of a horse when she got on its back.

"Take her around the track a time or two, Serilda, to warm her up. We'll all be watching," Pa smiled encouragingly.

"And keep her head up," Katie called as Serilda and Star rode away.

Serilda rode out into the ring. She let Star walk while she got the feel of things, then Star broke into an easy canter. Suddenly a shining black horse came pounding up beside them and Star began to prance as Colonel Thompson reined alongside and tipped his hat. "Well, we meet again, Miss Serilda. Glad to see you and your fine mare. Quite a few entries today. Your first time, isn't it? And you are our only lady, too. I wish you the best of luck."

For a few minutes the black stallion and the sorrel mare were side by side again, the stallion blowing his breath in quick sharp snorts and curving his shining body. Then the Colonel rode away. Serilda felt a sudden sinking in her heart as the man at the stand lifted the horn.

"Best riding horse, shown by owner. Will all riders please line up their mounts before the judges' stand." There were nine of them.

Serilda tried to remember as they started out, but her mind was whirling. Back and forth, around the ring, one by one, the judges had them walk, trot, and canter. It finally narrowed down to three, Black Chief, a high-stepping bay, and Star. Out front the judges had the three line up. Serilda sat straight, her heart pounding. Star stood motionless as the judges walked around each horse, debating. They came to Star and looked her over carefully, felt of the long scar on her leg. Then after more talk among themselves, they went to Black Chief and tied the blue ribbon on his bridle, the red ribbon on the bridle of the bay. Star got nothing at all.

Serilda held back the tears until she was out of the ring and back to the buggy where Pa and Jeff and Katie had hurried to help her get ready for the driving contest soon to follow.

"We didn't get a thing, not a thing," Serilda said brokenly as she slid off of Star's back.

"You almost got something. You were one of the last three. The judges had a hard time deciding," Katie said as she helped Serilda unhook her skirt. Then she took a cloth to help Jeff wipe the sweat from Star.

Pa put the harness on Star's back. "Star is a better buggy horse than a saddle horse and you're a better driver than a rider. Now with Black Chief it's the other way round; he's better under the saddle," he said as he buckled the bellyband and let the buggy shafts down over Star's back and fastened the tugs. "Remember, Colonel Thompson and some of the others are old hands at showing off their horses. You did fine for the first time. Made Ma and me right proud, Serilda." There was a warm, comforting look in his eyes.

"And this time, do as they say," Jeff warned. "Once you turned left when they said right. You made Star lope when she should have trotted. You were slow changing her gaits, too. Why, the Colonel and the bay's rider changed their horses from a trot to a lope just like that," Jeff snapped his fingers.

Serilda felt limp, heartsick. How could she ever go back to the ring and face the crowd? She and Star would just get beaten again. Maybe if she asked Pa he would let her off. For an instant the words trembled on her lips; then a hot shamed feeling swept over her. Pa, whose word the neighbors said was good as gold! And Pa had paid the entry fee and she had signed her name, like a pledge. She knew in her heart that she had to drive, but there was a dry tightness in her throat and a lump she could not swallow.

"I think this first time was like practicing," Pa said as if he knew her thoughts. "You've got the hang of it now. Maybe you were afraid of Black Chief, too, after seeing him jump the gate. But don't you worry about any other horse. You just think about Star."

Serilda turned to Star and looked at her. She was as sleek and shining as a new copper, white legs spotless. It wasn't Star's fault she didn't win. She leaned against Star and Star nuzzled her shoulder softly, loving her.

Suddenly Katie unfastened the locket from around her neck and fastened it around Serilda's. "For good luck," she said softly. "And don't let Black Chief or any of the others scare you. Just pretend we're in the pasture, and, when they say trot, get out in front and let Star go!"

Pa flicked a last spot of dust from the buggy and Serilda took a long, deep breath and climbed in. She picked up the lines and tried to smile at the three anxious faces.

"We'll all be watching," Pa said as she spoke to Star and started for the ring.

Colonel Thompson drove in just ahead of her, Black Chief hitched to a fine new buggy. The high-stepping bay was there, too. Then Serilda felt her heart sink as she saw the dapple gray, with the plumy white mane and tail, flashing around the ring, the new buggy glistening in the sunshine. Suddenly Serilda was very conscious of every squeak and rattle in the old buggy, of the harness they had tried so bravely to make shine with beeswax. It would be even worse than the riding.

She glanced over at the fence and there was the family. Pa holding little Bill up on his shoulder so he could see, Ma and the others close beside him.

"Best single driving horse, shown by owner," the man with the horn announced. "Walk your horses around the ring." The same men were judging.

Serilda slowed Star instantly to a walk. Around the ring they went, single file, Black Chief ahead, Star next, stepping as proudly as any thoroughbred, her neck arched, her brown eyes alert and shining, muscles rippling under the smooth sorrel coat, her trim little ears pointed ahead. Pa was right, Star was better hitched to a buggy than under a saddle. The buggy and harness might look shabby, but there was surely nothing wrong with the horse. Serilda sat up straight and confidence slowly came back to her as she drove around the ring. Star responded to the slightest signal as if she could read Serilda's wishes through the lines.

"Let 'em trot," came the crisp order.

Serilda spoke to Star and pulled up beside Black Chief, trotting side by side like a team. Then Serilda heard the slash of a whip and a rush as the dapple gray, breathing hard, was cutting by them, wanting the lead. Suddenly Katie's words flashed before her, "Get out in front and let Star go!" Serilda felt a fierce pride sweep over her. She loosened the lines and spoke to Star. And Star answered. The white legs flashed until they blurred with speed, the silky mane and tail floated in the wind. The old buggy almost slid around the curves and Serilda braced her feet and leaned to the inside to keep it balanced. The dapple gray dropped back; even Black Chief took second place. Around the ring, once, twice, and Star's swift trot never faltered, not once did she break her stride.

Serilda was proud enough to burst. "Step high! You're goin' good! Show 'em how fine you are!" Her voice full of love and pride flowed softly to

Star, and Star swiveled her little pointed ears and gave a tiny snort for an answer.

Then they had to walk their horses, turn right, turn left, and make more trips around the ring before they were stopped in front of the judges' stand.

Star stood square, like a bronze statue, neck bowed and tail arched, ears pricked forward, Black Chief and the dapple gray on either side, the others down the line. Serilda could hardly breathe as the judges walked around the horses, measuring, looking, debating.

The dapple gray pawed restlessly, tossing his head, and Black Chief moved nervously as the judges took their time.

Prickles ran up and down Serilda's arms as she held the lines and looked straight ahead. There was some talk of the scar on Star's leg, and if that should count against her.

When it seemed she could stand it no longer, one of the judges walked over and fastened the blue ribbon to Star's bridle, right by Grandma's red tassel. Then he smiled at Serilda and handed her a little blue box tied with a blue ribbon. "You made it this time, young lady; here is the award of ten dollars in gold. Congratulations." He gave Star an admiring pat and then turned to Black Chief.

"First place and ten dollars in gold goes to Miss Serilda Shaw, and her sorrel mare, Star—the first young lady ever to compete in the saddle and harness division. Second place to Colonel Thompson and his thoroughbred, Black Chief."

Out in front the crowd cheered and yelled and Serilda's face flushed with pleasure. Colonel Thompson and the driver of the gray horse smiled and tipped their hats to her, as Colonel Thompson said, "Miss Serilda, you've the finest little mare in the county and you drove her like an old hand. Black Chief and I have no regrets, losing to two such fair ladies. Our congratulations."

Serilda wanted to laugh and shout, but she held it back and thanked the Colonel as dignified as any grownup. Ma would expect her to. Then the judge dismissed them, and Serilda and Star, leading the line, went once more around the ring, the blue ribbon shining for all to see, the little blue box tucked safely in Serilda's pocket.

CHAPTER 12

Star Is Recognized

JEFF WAS waiting at the gate as Serilda drove out of the ring. He jumped into the buggy beside her. "Star beat the Chief! She beat the Chief! And you've ten dollars in gold! You're rich! What are you goin' to do with all that money?"

Serilda, flushed and excited, guided Star back toward the wagon. "If Pa and Ma don't care, I'm going to give half to Katie to buy her books and help pay her schooling. The rest I'll keep and, if Star really does have a little colt, I'll buy it a bridle."

Jeff let out a low whistle. "Wouldn't it be 'frazzlin' fine' to own a colt of Star's sired by Black Chief! The two best driving horses in the county!"

Serilda's smile spread across her face.

Pa and Katie were waiting at the wagon, but Ma and Grandma and little Bill went by the tent to look again at the quilts and handwork. Tib and Tony neighed as Star came up beside them.

"Star's got a bragging look in her eyes," Pa grinned as he helped Serilda from the buggy. "It's a big day for the Shaws," he said. "Two blue ribbons and twenty dollars in gold, and, to top it off, Ma won the parlor lamp for best coverlid."

It was a grand, big day, Serilda agreed as she rubbed Star's face and slipped her an apple from the dinner basket.

She noticed Katie standing a little apart, her face white and drawn, a worried look in her blue eyes. Serilda hurried to her.

"Katie, are you sick and having chills again?"

Katie shook her head. "I'm not sick," she leaned close to Serilda, her voice low. "While you were showing Star, I spied two men I'd seen before in Illinois. Horse traders like Paw. They've been to our camp. They knew Paw when he traded for Star. They follow after fairs and auctions and places where folks gather. They're just like Paw. When I saw them watching Star, oh, Serilda, I got such a terrible feeling." Suddenly Katie's eyes widened. "Hush! Here they come now."

Serilda turned to see two men walking toward them, eying Tib and Tony and then Star. One was short and heavy-set, with a rolling walk, brown hair and beard. The other tall and lean, with a slight limp and a long scar, like Star's, across his cheek. A battered hat shaded his eyes. Their clothes were rough and wrinkled and they wore square-toed boots with heavy stitching. They looked at the blue ribbon on Star's bridle and at Jeff, rubbing her down with a cloth.

Serilda caught her breath as fear swept across her. She stepped close to Pa and put her hand on Star's bridle.

The short man stuck out a broad, thick hand to Pa. "Howdy! My name's Busher and my pardner here is Slim Ruddy. We buy and trade horses. Nice team of draft horses ye got there. And the sorrel mare, she's right nice, too."

"Thanks," Pa said proudly as he shook hands. "The team is mine, brought in from the East, but the mare belongs to my daughter, Serilda."

Busher looked at Serilda admiringly. "We saw ye a drivin' her in the ring. Ye and the mare both done right well." Serilda barely nodded.

Busher looked from Serilda to Pa as if weighing something in his mind. "Ye know, me and Slim thinks we seen this mare before, back in Illinois. With them markin's a feller couldn't hardly mistake her. That 'un had a game leg, too. Same leg, same side, only must have got a heap worse, leavin' a scar like that. We wuz jist a ponderin' how ye come by her."

The thin one squatted down and peered at the scar on Star's leg. Serilda pulled on Pa's sleeve, but Pa felt expansive and smiled down at his daughter.

"Well, you see my daughter is sort of a horse trader, too," Pa chuckled teasingly. "She swapped her gold locket to a mover for the mare."

Busher stared at Serilda.

"And at the time," Pa continued, "I felt sure the mover got the best of the bargain. The mare was a pack of skin and bones and nigh dead with this running sore on her leg. Fact is, she was so bad the mover was ready to shoot her and skin her for the hide. Serilda got there just in the nick of time to save her."

Slim had been listening and the men exchanged glances. "Wuz his name Sam Wilson?" Busher asked.

"That's the name!" Pa said in amazement.

Busher turned to Serilda. "Did ye trade even? No boot?"

Serilda nodded, her heart in her throat.

"Have ye got anything to prove that ye traded even? That the mare is really yourn? Any writin'? Any papers? Any witnesses?"

Pa bristled. "We haven't any writin' but we have an eyewitness, the best you'd want. Wilson's own stepdaughter. She lives with us now. Katie, step over here."

Katie came slowly forward and Busher's eyes widened in recognition. "Why, ye rode herd for him, didn't ye?"

Katie nodded and took a deep breath. Then she told about Star and the trip from Illinois . . . "And we finally camped down by the covered bridge and the horse couldn't go any farther. Paw decided to shoot her and had the rifle and was walking toward her when Serilda came along from school. She swapped her locket for the horse"—Katie reached up and touched the locket around Serilda's neck— "and this is the locket. Maw got it from Paw and she gave it to me, and today Serilda wore it for good luck. The horse is Serilda's, fair and square, and that is the truth," Katie finished firmly, her face white with determination.

Serilda looked at the two men triumphantly. Nobody could doubt Katie's honesty. The horse was hers!

But Busher wasn't through. "Did yer paw ever mention the fact that the mare might be a thorough-bred? Did ye see any papers about her?"

Serilda caught her breath.

"He had some papers he kept locked in a box, but Paw couldn't read or write and he wouldn't know, only what somebody would tell him. Maw and me never saw 'em."

Katie shrugged her shoulders and looked up at the two men. "Paw said she was a thoroughbred, but he said that about lots of horses he traded for—that weren't." Katie flushed, ashamed, but she looked straight at the two men.

Busher grunted. "Wilson stretched things ter fit his fancy, but I think he told the truth this time. Jist look at that mare struttin' out there in the show ring. Mebbe she ain't all thoroughbred, but there's good blood there. It always tells. There's two or three breedin' farms of thoroughbreds in Illinois. I'll bet ye if Wilson ever sees 'er ag'in he'll want to kick hisself clean from here ter Jericho. Best mare he ever owned and he traded 'er off fer a trinket!" He burst out into a loud laugh and Slim made a wry face.

"But he did see . . ." Serilda started to say and then stopped short, but the men did not notice.

Busher took another look at Star and turned to go, bumping into a short, dwarfish man that had come up quietly behind him. He grabbed the man by the shoulder and cursed angrily. "What ye doin' here? Told ye to stay with the horses! How we goin' to do any tradin' if nobody's there ter talk to 'em?"

Serilda did not hear the little man's answer, but she caught the long, measuring look he gave Star before he followed Busher into the crowd.

"They call him Runty," Katie said as the men went out of sight. "He rides herd for them, same as I did for Paw. He used to be a jockey, so Paw said, but quit for some reason or other."

Serilda's heart was a tumult of joy and fear. She smoothed Star's forelock and looked deep into her soft brown eyes. Then she untied the blue ribbon and held it carefully.

"Pa, nobody can ever take Star away from me, can they?"

"Nobody," Pa said firmly. "But after today we'll

write out a paper and have Katie sign it as an eye-witness to the trade. Then I think we'll ask Colonel Thompson how to find out if Star really is a thoroughbred."

"If she isn't, I'll love her just the same. Anyway, she is the best driving horse in Livingston County and maybe the whole state of Missouri!"

Jeff unhitched Star and tied her to the wagon.

"Come on, let's go see something beside horses. Pa, can't we stay till dark? There's things here we'll never have a chance to see again. The cows can go without milkin' just once, can't they?"

Pa grinned. "Go on, we won't worry about the cows till we get home. I'll find Ma and Grandma and tell them we will stay late."

With a whoop Jeff grabbed Katie and Serilda and started running.

CHAPTER 13

Katie's First Day of School

SERILDA was dreaming of a pasture full of little colts that all looked like Star, when Katie shook her. "Serilda, wake up! It's coming daylight. I hear your Paw fixing the fire and your Maw's up, too. It's the first day of school. Remember?" She jumped out of bed and began to dress.

"Oh, Serilda, I'm so worked up. It's upsettin' to be goin' to a real school for the first time in your life— to have a new Fifth Reader and Speller and Arithmetic. Even copy paper and a quill pen. I'm singing inside with thankfulness.

"An' I'm so obliged to you for dividin' the fair money, and to your paw for the quinine that broke the chills and fever, and to your maw for making the new dress, and to Star for bringing us together! Serilda, I couldn't shut my eyes the whole blessed night for thinking about today and how I'm going to study and learn every single thing in the books." She stopped for breath.

Serilda frowned and looked sleepily at Katie. "That sure was a long speech to make before breakfast. I don't think you will have to worry about learning the books. You have been poring over 'em every spare minute since Pa brought 'em home." Serilda got up and fumbled for her pantalets and petticoat.

It was quiet for a moment, then Katie spoke slowly, "Do you think they will poke fun at me because I've always been a mover?"

Serilda was suddenly wide awake. "Humph! All the old folks were movers. That's how they got here. If anybody pokes fun at you, they'll sure shut up when you stand up to spell and read and figger. Besides that, you know more about horses than anybody else in the whole county, unless it might be Colonel Thompson."

Katie burst out laughing, a relieved look on her face. "Serilda, I think you'll turn into a horse sometime."

"Just so it's a thoroughbred, I don't care." Serilda laughed, too, as they hurried out to help Ma with breakfast.

Later, Star harnessed to the buggy, a bag of oats under the seat, the dinner pails packed, books and slates in a cloth bag, they were ready for school.

Ma and Grandma and little Bill stood in the door to watch them leave.

"I'm right proud of the three of you," Ma said as she looked at Serilda in her Sunday blue calico and blue bonnet, and Katie in her new red dress and bonnet to match, the locket around her neck. Jeff, too, was spruce in a blue cotton shirt and linsey-woolsey pants, his boots shiny with tallow.

Serilda picked up the lines and clucked to Star.

"Drive slow," Jeff pleaded. "I want to see how the men are gettin' along with the mill. Last week they had the forebay all finished and the floor down to the mill. The forebay is like a cellar under the mill, with the river runnin' through it. It's got a gate on each end to let the water in and let it out. There's a big, old stout pole stuck right through the mill floor with wooden paddles on the bottom end in the forebay. And fastened to that pole, above the paddles and underneath the floor are big wooden cog wheels to turn the second set of stone burrs in the room above. They've two sets of burrs to grind coarse and fine.

"When they open the gates and that old river pours in and hits the paddles and the cogs turn and the burrs begin to grind—that's goin' to be somethin' to see and hear!

"I'll bet it'll be the biggest gristmill between here and Brunswick, and folks will come from all over everywhere to get their grain ground. They're going to make a dam across the river, too, so they'll always have water to run the mill." He gave a long deep sigh. "Sure does seem a shame to have to go to school when there's so much interestin' goin' on."

"Nothing on earth could be as interesting as going to school," Katie said in a shocked voice.

Serilda laughed. "Well, you two can talk about your interesting things, but I'm saying this is what I like best in the whole world." She made a sweeping motion that included everything. "Trees all red and yellow and the sky blue as indigo. White clouds floating here and there and silver cobwebs drifting, thin like. Persimmons and pawpaws and hickory nuts and walnuts falling on the ground, and all the wild things building nests for the winter. Old Indian Hill all blue and hazy and everything kinda still and waiting. And Star and us right here in the middle! I wish it would stay October forever and ever!"

They were suddenly quiet as they looked across the valley.

"It's like the pickled crabapples your maw had for supper last night—sweet and sour, both," Katie said finally. "The trees and bushes blazin' with so much color are plumb lovely, but it makes you ache, too, with a lonesomeness, way down deep inside." She looked thoughtfully into the distance. "Maw used to say October pleasured her eyes and saddened her heart," she added wistfully.

"I think it would pleasure her heart this year, knowing you were feeling fine and going to school," Serilda said as they passed the covered bridge and came to the log where Katie had studied. "A year ago you were sitting on that log wishing you could go to school with me. And now you are!"

[121]

"And you were wishing you could have a horse and now you have one and, come next June, maybe you will have two," Katie said happily.

Serilda looked at Star and lovingly rubbed the lines across her back. She whistled softly and Star flicked her ears and gave a quick little nicker.

"Maybe in a few years we will all have a horse to ride," Jeff chuckled.

Boys were playing in the schoolyard and, after Star was unhitched, Jeff joined them, but Serilda and Katie went to the schoolhouse.

Mr. Moss was waiting at the door to greet the pupils.

"This is my friend, Katie Briggs," Serilda said proudly. "She lives at our house now and she is coming to school with us. She likes books as much as I do horses."

Mr. Moss smiled and shook hands with Katie. "Then you will be a fine scholar, for Serilda surely loves her horses. We're very glad to have you."

"It pleasures me to be here," Katie said in a proper, grown-up manner.

They stepped inside and Serilda put the dinner pail on the shelf with the others. Several girls were already there and looked curiously at Katie. Lucy Denton motioned to Serilda and Katie.

"The seat in front of me is not taken; come and sit

there. Haven't seen you since the fair. Did you drive that blue ribbon horse to school? Or are you afraid something will happen to her?"

She rattled on. "It sure is nice to have Mr. Moss back again instead of some stranger. He's boarding with us the first six weeks. He came on the train clear from Indiana. He wants to get the Literary Society started right away and says he is going to have a spelling match, or a ciphering match every Friday after the last recess. And the one that wins the most times gets a prize at the end of school."

Lucy stopped suddenly as she saw Katie's new Fifth Reader. "Can you read in that? I didn't think that movers could read and write. They never go to school."

"They can read and write and spell and figger, too," Serilda said shortly.

Katie's face flushed and she turned to Lucy. "My maw swapped for some books and taught me. She is real smart. I studied alongside the road while I tended the horses," she said quietly.

"And someday she's going to be a schoolteacher!" Serilda said triumphantly. She reached under the desk and squeezed Katie's hand.

"A schoolteacher? Well, I never . . ." And before Lucy could think it over, Mr. Moss rang the bell, and big and little boys trooped in, jostling and scuffling as they found their seats.

Katie was the only stranger there and everyone knew that she was a mover, living with the Shaws. They eyed her curiously when she walked up front with Serilda and the others for the reading class; the room grew quiet as prayer time. Serilda could feel Katie trembling as she stood close beside her, but when it was Katie's turn to read her voice was firm and clear and she read the whole lesson with only one mistake. Mr. Moss was surprised and said, "Very good. Very good."

In spelling, Katie spelled the words so quickly and easily that Mr. Moss gave her a try in the advanced class that was starting in the middle of the book and she spelled every word correctly. Serilda caught Jeff's eye and they grinned at each other.

Later in the day, when it came time to do the sums and Mr. Moss sent the class to the blackboard and gave them a problem in long division, Katie was the last to finish and the answer was incorrect. When she returned to her seat, her face was so flushed Serilda worried that the fever might be coming back.

In the back of the room someone laughed and Serilda turned to glare at them, but Katie stared straight ahead, a determined look on her face.

"I lost my wits, trying to figger while everybody watched," Katie said grimly as Mr. Moss rang the bell for dismissal. "There is such a lot to learn and it's not all in the books, either."

Katie read the whole lesson

Jeff decided to walk home with the Denton boys and Serilda asked Lucy to ride in his place. Star pranced and snorted as they hitched her to the buggy and Jeff had to hold her as the girls got in. Then she was off.

"Makes you feel high-toned to ride in a buggy behind such a 'git-up-and-go' horse," Lucy said, as Star set off at a brisk trot, her mane and tail flying in the breeze. "You're lucky," she looked at Katie slyly, "you wear the locket and ride behind the horse, too."

Serilda never said a word, but she shoved back her bonnet and loosened the lines and Star took them so fast over the rutty road that Lucy squealed and gave up trying to talk.

"I guess that is one way to shut her up." Katie laughed ruefully as Lucy got out of the buggy and they started home.

"Pay no mind to her, she just gabs both ways for Sunday! Before the term is out she will be bragging about you. Katie, I'll bet you get the prize at the end of school for being the best speller."

"I'm surely going to try," Katie said. "Maw would be proud of that."

At home they took off their Sunday dresses and changed into everyday ones. Katie unfastened the locket, too, and put it in the little velvet box in Grandma's bureau. Serilda, watching, knew it was Lucy's remark that caused it.

That night Jeff and Katie and Serilda sat around the long table with Ma's lamp shining brightly in the center. Katie studied spelling and practiced sums on her slate until she almost went to sleep. Serilda practiced sums, too, but at the top of the slate she drew a picture of a horse with a star in her forehead and around the edge a fancy border of little colts.

CHAPTER 14

Star Is Missing

SERILDA awoke to the sound of rain beating against the bedroom window and the moan of the wind as it whipped around the house and through the treetops. The gray light of early morning filled the room where a coldness had seeped in during the night. The fine October weather had ended and the first breath of winter had swept over the hills.

Serilda listened for a moment, and heard Ma stirring corn cakes for breakfast, then she snuggled down under the covers close to Katie, thankful it was Saturday and that there would be no school—hoping Ma would let them sleep late.

She was just drifting off again when she heard Pa come in from outside and begin talking to Ma. Then he walked to the stairway and called Jeff and told him to hurry. Something in Pa's voice brought Serilda wide awake, and Katie stirred and raised up on her elbow and looked questioningly at Serilda.

Ma came to the bedside, a worried look on her face. "Girls, you'll have to get up and help Pa and Jeff. Somebody took the fence down during the night and let the stock out of the pasture. Here's some of

Jeff's old jeans. Try and squeeze into them. You'd ruin your dresses clambering through the woods."

Serilda bounced out of bed. "I'll ride Star. We can round them up in a hurry."

Ma cleared her throat. "Tib and Tony and the oxen were waiting at the gate to be let into the barn, but Star wasn't with them. She is gone, too, Serilda."

"Star gone? Ma, she can't be gone!" Serilda choked on the words, her mouth suddenly dry as flour. "She's always first at the barn gate to get her feed!"

Ma shook her head. "She's gone, Daughter. And the cows are all gone, too, and that heifer that just freshened will be in a bad way if she isn't milked by noon. Get into your things. You'll have to eat some breakfast before you start out." Ma turned back to the kitchen.

Katie had been flying into her things while they were talking, but Serilda was shaking so she could hardly fasten her shoes.

"Katie, do you think anybody would try to steal Star?"

"No one with a lick of sense! After everybody saw her at the fair, why, she's known all over the county! She is the same as Black Chief!"

"But they could hide her in the daytime and ride her at night."

Katie gave Serilda a quick hug. "Don't go borrowing trouble. We'll find her. Maybe she lamed herself in the woods or got caught in a thorny thicket. When she hears you whistle, she'll come."

Serilda choked over her breakfast. The corn cakes stuck tight in her throat and had to be washed down with swallows of milk.

Pa talked between bites. "When the cows and Star weren't waiting at the gate, I put Tib and Tony in their stalls and went to look for them. I covered the whole pasture and that is when I found the place where the fence was down, over at the far side next to the woods. The four top rails had been let down, and there were tracks at one end, horse tracks and cattle tracks—and now and then big boot tracks. All faintlike, so it must have happened in the middle of the night when it first began to storm and the rain washed over them."

Jeff stole glances at Serilda as he ate and Grandma kept urging everyone to eat more ham and honey with their corn cakes to keep them warm out in the storm.

At last Pa pushed back from the table. "Jeff, go over to Dentons' and ask if they've seen anything unusual. Then come right home. The girls and I will take Grover and follow the tracks as far as we can. When you get back, come down in the woods and follow along and keep hollering. We'll hear you and answer. I don't see how we can miss finding the cows, but Old Shortie, she's a smart one for hiding out."

Pa got up and went to the fireplace and reached up over the mantle for his Kentucky rifle. Serilda could see the muscles working in his jaw. There was no twinkle in his eyes today.

Wrapped in heavy jackets and hoods, Serilda and Katie walked with Pa across the pasture, leaning against the wind. Serilda carried Star's bridle on her arm. The rain had turned to sleet that stung like needles as the wind flung it in their faces. They came to the place where the fence had been taken down and they bent over looking at the tracks, now getting dim in the covering of sleet.

Serilda straightened and gave the shrill familiar whistle that always brought an answering neigh from Star. They stood, motionless, listening, but there was no answer. Serilda whistled again and again, but the only sound was the creaking and sighing of the icy tree limbs and the beating of sleet against the fence rails.

Pa signaled to Grover. "Go get the cows! Find the cows!"

Grover sniffed for a moment and struck off at a lope, following the trail into the woods. Pa and Serilda and Katie hurried after him.

It was an easy trail to follow for broken branches and fresh droppings marked the way. Serilda whistled often and they stopped to listen, but no answering neigh came to them.

Pa's frown was deeper and Serilda tried to swallow the lump of fear that grew bigger and bigger. She searched the tracks carefully to be sure that Star's was still among them. Katie and Pa watched for the bootprints and Pa said, "Awful short steps for such big feet."

Startled rabbits scurried from their nests and quail whirred up in sudden flight and a deer bounded through the brush ahead of them, but not once did Pa bring his gun to shoulder.

They stopped to rest on a fallen log, for it was slick under foot and tiresome going. The sleet was changing to big, wet flakes of snow and the wind was dying. Serilda's lips felt stiff from whistling, but once again she sent out the shrill call to Star, and they held their breath to listen. Suddenly Grover began barking frantically.

Serilda's heart jumped and she started plunging through the brush toward the barking, Pa and Katie close behind. They came out in a little open space in a curve of the creek, sheltered from the wind by a rocky cliff. There was Old Shortie and all the other cattle, chewing their cuds, unmindful of the storm. Star was not with them.

Far off in the distance they heard Jeff calling and Pa answered.

The two oldest Denton boys, Charley and Jim, were with Jeff, ready to help in the search. Jeff's eyes swept the herd of cattle; then he looked at Serilda. She shook her head and moved the empty bridle in her hand, trying to hide the aching disappointment in her heart.

"We haven't seen a thing," the oldest boy said to Pa. "Along in the night the dogs set up an awful howling and barking, like they do when somebody is passing, but that's all. My father said, if you needed him he'd come."

"Much obliged," Pa said tiredly, leaning for a minute against a tree. Everyone waited for Pa to speak and the stock began moving restlessly as Grover walked around the edge.

Then Pa pulled his coonskin cap farther down on his forehead, squared his shoulders, and shifted the rifle in the crook of his arm.

"Jeff, you and Jim and Katie take the stock back to the barn and do the milking. Charley, you and Serilda and I will take Grover and keep following the trail until we find Star, or lose the trail. If it keeps on snowing, that won't be long."

With the cattle headed back toward the barn, Serilda held Star's bridle by Grover's nose. "Star . . . Star . . . Star," she said over and over. Grover looked up into her face and she dropped a mittened hand on either side of his face and looked straight into his eyes. "Go find Star! Go find Star!" she commanded.

Grover wagged his tail and started out, but the cattle had trampled the ground in the little clearing and the creek bank until all scent of Star was lost.

Serilda followed wearily along the edge of the creek, her eyes searching for a broken twig, or a hoof-print, stopping often to whistle. Pa and Charley walked to one side, Grover running ahead. Pa said Star must have been ridden in the creek to hide her footprints. It seemed hours before the trail was found again, the boot tracks gone.

Now they walked single file, Pa leading the way. The creek was widening and they were nearing the main road that went past Dentons' and on to Red Oaks school, when Grover set up a furious barking at the end of a hollow log.

"Come out of there," Pa yelled angrily, but Grover only barked more frantically, crawling so far into the log that only his hind legs and wildly waving tail stuck out.

"He's stuck," Pa said disgustedly and hurried to grab Grover by the hind legs.

"A rabbit or a possum," Charley said as he stood ready, but when Grover's head came in sight they gasped in amazement, for Grover was holding on to a muddy, square-toed boot, with horseshoes stitched in red! Then before they could stop him, he dropped the boot and dived back into the log again. Pa pulled him out with another muddy boot in his mouth, the mate to the first one!

Serilda stared at them and gave a sharp cry. "Pa! They are Busher's boots! I remember the funny toes and the horseshoes stitched in red. The other man had boots just like them only they had a blue star for trimming. Oh, Pa! They stole my Star! They knew she was a thoroughbred. They'll take her back to Illinois and I'll never, never see her again!" Serilda slumped against Pa and dry, tearing sobs shook her body. Pa put his arm around her and said nothing, his mouth a hard, straight line.

Charley dropped to his knees and peered into the log, but there was nothing more. Grover, knowing something was wrong, watched Serilda and Pa with puzzled eyes.

"What I can't figger," Charley said as he looked at the muddy, worn boots, "is why would a feller throw away his boots and go barefoot this kind of weather. Don't make sense, even if they do have holes in the soles."

Pa shook his head. "I don't know, Charley, but we are going to find out. You carry the boots and we will go as long as we can see a hoofprint. Something tells me we will lose the trail when we come to the road, and it's not far from here."

Pa was right. The hoofprints were lost in the mixture of wagon tracks, and tracks of horses, cattle, and deer. Grover lost the trail, too.

"I'll take the boots now," Pa said. "Then we'll go home and I'll hitch up and drive to the county seat and tell the sheriff what has happened. Might be he could catch up with these scoundrels before they get clean away."

"Why don't you come up to our house and get Prince, our riding horse?" Charley suggested. "He'll make it in half the time your heavy team will. He is in the barn and I can saddle him in a jiffy. Serilda can ride home behind you."

At the Dentons' they went inside and, while Pa was telling about Busher and Ruddy at the fair and Star's being gone, Mrs. Denton dished them up a bowl of hot soup and gave Grover a chunk of johnnycake.

By the time Pa had finished, Mr. Denton was pulling on his cap and jacket. "I'll ride east to Rutherfords' and tell them and then one of them can go on and we'll get the news around. You can't get a horse like that out of the country without somebody seeing her." He sounded so positive, and that, with the hot soup, made Serilda feel better. She got up on Prince behind Pa and, with Grover trotting beside them, they started home.

CHAPTER 15

An Answer to the Sheriff's Letter

COLONEL THOMPSON, hearing the news about Star, offered money for a reward and got other donors, saying not a horse in the county was safe. Pa and all the neighbors did their part.

The sheriff had handbills printed. They were posted in stores in Spring Hill and Chillicothe and tacked to trees along the roads and one on each end of the covered bridge. There was one tacked on Red Oaks school and Serilda read it every day, a terrible sinking in her heart:

REWARD

STOLEN—from the pasture of Will Shaw, in Livingston County, Missouri, at the top of the hill by the covered bridge.

ONE SORREL MARE, eight years old, four white stockings, white star in forehead. Long scar on right foreleg. Answers to name of Star. $50 in gold for return of mare, safe and sound. $50 in gold for capture and conviction of thief.

Signed: J. W. Green, Sheriff

Other handbills with a description of Busher and Ruddy were mailed or sent to sheriffs in other counties and to the big towns along the rivers.

It was nearly two weeks later that the sheriff received a letter and brought it out to the Shaws' that evening. It was from the sheriff in Marion County. He read it aloud to the Shaws.

"Located Busher and Ruddy in Hannibal on the Mississippi River. They are working in a livery stable and doing a little horse trading on the side. They have been there three weeks. The owner of the stable vouched for that. Busher said he bought some new boots and threw his old ones away. He thinks Runty Pearson, the little man that had been with them, might have picked them up. They had a falling-out and Runty left. Said he was going back to Indiana where he came from. Busher doubts that, for he said Runty didn't dare go back. They haven't seen him since."

"So it wasn't Busher and Ruddy that took the mare," the sheriff said thoughtfully as he stared into the fire.

"Runty, how about him?" Pa asked. "He knew all about Star and looked at her awful straight at the fair. He heard them talking that maybe she was a thoroughbred. And the steps in the woods were awful short for such big feet. Maybe he wore the boots for overshoes. And maybe he didn't go back East but came here to get Star."

"How could he get clear back from Hannibal in two days. It's a hundred and fifty miles, isn't it? Kill a horse to ride that hard," Jeff said.

"He could ride on the train. It comes straight through from Hannibal," the sheriff said. "But I talked with the conductor and he said nobody answering that description rode the train from Hannibal. And the brakeman said he didn't catch any men trying to steal a ride. Just a half-grown boy that got away."

The sheriff got up and looked at Serilda. "I won't stop trying to find your horse, and don't you stop hoping and praying." He shook hands with Pa, said good-by and stepped out into the night.

The room was very quiet. Katie picked up the books and carried them to the table to begin studying. Jeff went to the table, too, and opened his arithmetic. It was easy to study with Ma's parlor lamp to light the table, but Serilda sat hunched in her chair, staring into the fire, a hopeless ache in her heart. Little Bill toddled over and climbed into Serilda's lap and she held him close until he went to sleep.

Ma, busy with her mending, looked at Serilda and then back to her patches. Pa, too, stared unseeing into the fire, his face drawn. Grandma looked up from her knitting. "Serilda, child, you best tend to your lessons. To put your mind on one thing takes it off another. Worrying over lost things never found them. Not even horses."

Serilda walked slowly to the table and sat down. She picked up her speller and wrote the words on her slate and tried to remember them, but it was all a blur. She opened the geography book and turned to the map of Missouri. She put her finger on the place marked Hannibal and the one farther south marked St. Louis and she traced the Mississippi River that made the boundary between Missouri and Illinois. She looked at the territory to the west.

It was only a page in the geography book, but Serilda could see a long, long road that reached for endless miles, and on this road a sorrel, white-footed horse with a star on her forehead and a long red scar on her leg was being ridden by some stranger who neither cared nor loved her.

"It's been a whole month," Serilda said wearily, as she snuffed out the candle and got into bed. "Star could be in Illinois or Indiana, or on the road to Oregon or California. After what the sheriff said, I don't think she will ever be found." Serilda was quiet for several minutes before she spoke again, her voice husky.

"I was too smart and proud, wanting to show Star off before people. I wish I'd never, never taken her to the fair. Somebody saw her there and wanted her. Oh, Katie, if she does have a little colt, now I'll never see it." Serilda buried her face in the pillow and sobbed bitterly.

Katie snuggled close and put a comforting arm around her.

CHAPTER 16

Serilda Runs a Foot Race

THE COLD November days shortened and often it was dusk when Serilda and Katie and Jeff got home from school. By that time the men had stopped working on the mill and movers often had a campfire going in the clearing and supper cooking.

Since the railroad had come to Chillicothe and the covered bridge was built, more and more strangers were being seen. Some of them were hunting a place to settle, others passing through on the long trail west. Often several families were traveling together, the white-covered wagons making slow-moving caravans. Pa said Chillicothe would live up to its name and be a big town sometime.

Today school had let out later than usual and Jeff had hurried on ahead to help Pa with the chores. There had been a spelling match, and Katie and Sam Rutherford had spelled so long without missing a word that it was after four when school was dismissed. But Katie won! And on the way home Lucy Denton told Katie she knew she could spell down anybody in the whole county.

"See what I told you," Serilda said jubilantly after Lucy left them. "She is bragging on you now, but you had to show her!"

Katie was jubilant, too. "I'm going to write to Maw tonight. The two or three lines I've been writing every few days have added up until I have a sheet of foolscap nearly full on both sides. If I don't hear from Maw pretty soon, I'll have to begin on another.

"It's been three months since I got that letter from Westport and they were ready to leave for Council Bluffs, Iowa. Wouldn't you think I'd get a letter by now? Every time I see a covered wagon I wonder where they are and if they're safe."

"I wouldn't worry, Katie. Going in a wagon train is lots safer than if they were alone. Maybe your mother has written but has no way to send the letter, or maybe it got lost," Serilda said. "Or it could be there is one waiting right now in the post office. Pa hasn't been for two weeks, but now he is through corn gathering, he'll go tomorrow."

"And maybe the sheriff will have some news about Star, too," Katie said hopefully.

Serilda did not answer as she walked along by Katie, the covered bridge ahead of them, dark against the evening sky.

All the days with Star flashed before her mind—the long trip up the hill when Star could barely move, the time she saved the bridge, and the first proud

[143]

walk across it, leading the parade, the flying trip to the doctor when Jeff cut his foot, Black Chief jumping the gate, and he and Star running side by side until they disappeared over the hill, the glorious blue-ribbon day at the fair, and all the days just loving her. Serilda stumbled a little over the rough places in the road, her eyes filled with tears.

"Katie, I don't think I'll ever see Star again. She is too far away by now. She might even be dead. It has been too long, nearly two months, and Colonel Thompson got that answer from the thoroughbred place in Illinois and they have nothing about her in their records. She is gone, Katie. Clear gone."

"But Colonel Thompson wrote to another place," Katie said quickly. "You mustn't give up. You know what your grandma says when she has a tooth pulled. Just when she thinks she is going to die, the tooth comes out!"

Serilda grinned and wiped away the tears. Katie had troubles of her own and never complained.

There were two wagons in the clearing and horses tethered close by. Children were running around and women were getting supper over the campfire, men unloading boxes from the wagons. Another covered wagon with four horses hitched to it was starting up the approach to the bridge, evidently going farther for the night.

"They are traveling awful late," Katie said as the

wagon rumbled into the bridge. "Paw always stopped early."

Suddenly a high, shrill whinny came from the bridge and echoed on the hills. The movers' horses threw up their heads and answered.

Serilda grabbed Katie by the arm and stopped, rigid.

"Star! It sounded like Star!"

Katie looked sadly at Serilda. "You're imagining things," she said and started on. "That horse was just saying 'Howdy' to these here at the camp site. They all do that. He's tired and wanting to stop."

Serilda started on slowly, the aching loneliness for Star back in her heart again. Then from over the river came the shrill, high whinny again. Serilda whirled and faced the sound, caught a deep breath, and gave the old familiar whistle. A high, joyous whinny came back and then another and another!

"It is Star! It is Star!" Serilda flung down the books and went tearing toward the bridge.

Katie grabbed at her and screamed, "Serilda, don't! Don't!" But Serilda kept on running and Katie dropped the dinner pail by the books and flew down the road after her.

Across the dark tunnel of the bridge Serilda raced, the wagon a dim spot disappearing in the twilight. She jerked up her long skirts to run faster. Once she stumbled and sprawled on the rough road and skinned her knees, but she jumped to her feet and ran on again. She cried out for the man to stop, but the wagon kept on moving.

"He's got to stop. Oh, God, help me to stop him!" Dry, tearing sobs came from her throat. Then, with the last bit of breath she screamed, "Stop! Stop! Stop!"

And the wagon stopped. A man and a woman leaned out, waiting for Serilda.

"My horse!" Serilda panted. "You've got my horse! I heard her whinny. I whistled and she answered!" Serilda leaned on the wheel, breathless and stared up into the astonished faces. "I can tell you what she's like without even looking. Four white stockings and a white star in her forehead and a long—"

"Little lady," the man broke in, "none of my horses got white legs. I'm trying to get to Spring Hill tonight and that's a far piece yet to go. I don't know where you live, maybe with them campers back there, but seems to me you better be getting home this time of night." He stared down at Katie as she suddenly appeared. "And you best go with her, too." He shifted the lines.

Serilda reached up and took hold of the woman's skirt. "You must listen," she begged. "I live at the top of the long hill with my folks. My grandma has lived there for thirty-five years. We are on our way

"Star, my Star! You're found!"

home from school and I heard Star whinny and I ran after her. She's got a long scar on her right front leg. She was stolen and there's a reward out for her."

"Stolen! Reward!" the man grunted in surprise.

The off front horse nickered again and Serilda and Katie ran around to look. There was a white star in the horse's forehead, but the forelock was shorn away and the mane clipped close to her neck. She looked strange, and yet familiar.

"Star? My Star?" Serilda reached out and rubbed the velvety nose and the horse gave a soft little fluttery nicker and nuzzled Serilda's shoulder. Serilda threw her arms around the horse's neck and hugged her with all her might. "It's you! You're found! You're found!" Star rubbed her face against Serilda and nipped the sleeve of her dress.

Katie squatted down and looked at the horse's legs. They were dark like the rest of her, but on the right front leg ran a long scar. Katie grabbed Serilda and pointed. The man had come from the wagon and stood behind them. "Her legs have been dyed, Serilda," Katie said excitedly. "Walnut hulls, probably. They changed her looks a heap, but they couldn't change that scar. It's Star! It sure is!"

"The man I got her from said he put stuff on her legs to keep off the flies. But she acts like she knows you, and she did try to turn in at the place at the top of the hill. But I have to have more evidence than that. I had a horse die in Brunswick and got this one to replace it. The receipt's right here in my pocket sayin' I bought her, and for how much, and the owner signed his name. Maybe she was your horse once, but she is sure mine now."

"Please come and talk to Pa," Serilda pleaded. "Maybe you do have papers to show you bought her, but she is my horse. Pa and the sheriff will know what to do."

"The sheriff," the man said sharply. "I want no dealin's with the law."

"But if you're innocent," Katie said quickly, "you've nothing to be feared of."

The man went to the wagon and talked with the woman in a low voice. It was almost dark now. A thin crescent of a moon hung over Indian Hill, and whippoorwills sang their mournful evening song. Serilda stood waiting, trembling, her hand on Star.

"We'll turn around and go back," the man said finally, "and get this straightened out. If we don't, I allow as how we'd be followed. I've never been mixed up with the law and don't intend to be. But it's too late to go on to Spring Hill tonight. Can we find a campin' spot at the top of the hill?"

"Oh, yes," Serilda said quickly, "and you can water your horses from our well."

"You girls want to ride?"

[149]

"No, much obliged," Serilda said. "We left our books and dinner pail by the bridge."

They waited until the man had the horses and wagon turned around and started back. They hurried over the bridge and felt around in the grass and weeds until they found the books and pail; then they went up the long, steep hill, walking by Star all the way. Nearly home they met Pa and Jeff and Grover. The dog set up such a barking and running and jumping in front of Star that Pa had to call him off.

"Pa, we've found Star! Look! She's right here by us!" Serilda sang out. "She whinnied and I heard her and then I whistled and she answered. She doesn't look like Star, but she is. The man wants it all straightened out and I told him you and the sheriff would know what to do," Serilda poured out the words.

Pa started to speak and then stopped as if he didn't know where to begin.

As they got nearer to the house, Star began to strain ahead and there was no need for the man to guide his horses, for, with quick, urgent steps, Star led them into the driveway. As they stopped, she gave a loud, joyous whinny that Tib and Tony out in the pasture answered and came trotting up to the gate. Star was home again.

As the man got down from the wagon, Pa was waiting. "I'm Will Shaw," he said.

"Benson's my name, Nate Benson. Got my wife and two little girls in the wagon. We're on our way to Spring Hill to visit the Stouts, kin of ours, before we go on to St. Joe." Pa nodded his head; he knew the Stouts.

"Your girl, here, she ran me down and says I'm driving her horse, and it's plain to be seen the horse knows her and this place. She says the mare was stolen, and something about a reward and you and the sheriff settling things, but it needs explaining. I paid forty dollars for this horse in Brunswick and I have a receipt to show for it, signed by R. B. Pearson, little short fellow with reddish hair. He left after he got the money. Got on a steamboat headed for St. Louis."

"Pearson!" Pa let out a low whistle. "I'll bet that half-grown boy the brakeman saw running across the railroad tracks was Runty. Benson, unhitch your horses and put them in the barn. Take a little time to thrash this out."

This was what Serilda had been waiting for. With flying fingers, she and Katie unhitched Star while Jeff helped the men with the other horses. The girls walked beside Star as she went to her old stall. In the darkness, Serilda leaned her head against Star and said a little prayer of thankfulness, but Katie was feeling Star's sides with practiced hands. "Serilda," she whispered, her voice shaking with excitement, "Star is going to have a colt. There's no doubt about it!"

Serilda caught her breath and was swept up in a wild rush of joy and tenderness. Star home and going to have a colt! A colt by Black Chief! Then Katie brought her down again with a jolt. "Serilda, Benson won't want to give her up without he can get another horse in her place and that will take money."

"We'll find a way," Serilda said fiercely. "Katie, we *have* to find a way."

Early the next morning Pa and Mr. Benson hitched Star up to the buggy and drove into town to see the sheriff. Ma and Mrs. Benson and Grandma worked and visited, and Katie and Serilda played with the little girls, but Serilda's mind wasn't on the playing. She was wondering every minute what Pa would have to tell when he returned.

When they came back, Serilda ran to the side of the buggy and looked up into Pa's face. "What did he say, Pa? Could he tell it was Star? Did he say she was mine now, just like before?"

Pa didn't answer at once, but got out of the buggy and tied Star to the hitchrack.

"Mr. Benson, did you tell him how she answered

when I whistled? And that was the way I found her?" Serilda had to know.

There was a worried frown on Mr. Benson's face, but he smiled when he looked down at Serilda. "Yes, we told him everything. Your friend, Colonel Thompson, was there, too. She is your horse all right. We all agreed to that." He took a deep breath. "I was sure lucky to have the receipt to show I actually bought her. But it leaves me in a tight place. Now I have to find another horse."

"Come on, let's go in the house," Pa said, "and we will tell the whole story." Serilda thought she caught a twinkle in his eyes. Everyone gathered around to listen.

"We went to the sheriff's and got Colonel Thompson and some others for witnesses. They all agreed that it was Star. They looked at Mr. Benson's receipt and agreed it was bona fide, too," Pa said. "And the sheriff said he would write immediately to the law officers in St. Louis and the other river towns to watch out for Runty. Nobody can figger out why he sold Star after coming clear back to get her and why he signed his own name to the receipt.

"Then there was another thing they all agreed on. The reward offered to the person finding Star and returning her to the owner, safe and sound, should go to you, Serilda."

Pa reached into his inside jacket pocket and took

out a little buckskin bag. Serilda took it, her fingers trembling. She pushed back the drawstring and poured the contents on the table—ten shining pieces of gold! Fifty dollars!

It was a fortune. She stared at it. That was enough for a new saddle, or half enough for the spring wagon Ma had been wanting so long. She caught her breath and looked around at Ma and Jeff and Katie and the Bensons. Such riches fairly took your breath! She tried to think what it all meant.

She stood for a minute, undecided, then she went to Pa and talked so low the others could not hear. "I don't feel we should take all the money. It is not right. Part of it is Mr. Benson's. I found Star, but Mr. Benson returned her safe and sound! He didn't have to; he could have gone right on down the road and never stopped. Pa, he's been good to Star. Let's give enough of it to him to buy another horse. Can't we, Pa?" She looked anxiously at Pa and there was a sudden mistiness in his eyes as he put his arm around her. He looked across at Ma and then at Mr. Benson.

"Tell Mr. Benson what you told me, Serilda," Pa said. And Serilda told him. Mr. Benson's face lit up like a flash of summer lightning and Mrs. Benson wiped her eyes.

"I know where you can probably get one for a lot less than forty dollars," Katie spoke up quickly.

"The movers camped down by the bridge are still there. I saw smoke from their campfire. They have a lot of extra horses. I saw them last night."

"Then let's go and make a trade," Pa said, and he and Mr. Benson went out of the door.

CHAPTER 17

The Book of Useful Knowledge

THE WINTER months slipped by and spring came on soft, warm winds, bringing a rainbow of wild flowers along the roadside and the green of new leaves across the hills. Overhead the wild ducks and geese winged their way back from the southland, and robins and blue jays found their old nesting places around the yard.

It was the end of March and the last day of the school term. Serilda and Katie and Jeff, walking home from school, felt like colts let out on fresh pasture. It had been a wonderful, exciting day. There had been oral reviews in everything, climaxed by a spelling match where Katie and Sam Rutherford battled it out for the last time. Dinner had been eaten together on a grassy spot in the yard, with a game of handball afterward.

Then Mr. Moss gave each pupil a fancy card with attendance and grade average for the year. That was something new. After that he announced that he was giving the award to the best speller of the year and everyone sat perfectly still. He picked up a thick, green-bound book with gold lettering.

[156]

"The Book of Useful Knowledge," he said and held it up for all to see. Then he opened the cover and read:

"Presented to Katie Briggs, for missing the fewest words and winning the most spelling matches during the school term at Red Oaks School, Livingston County, Missouri. March 1868.

> *Alexander Moss, Teacher"*

Everyone cheered and clapped, even Sam, as Katie went forward to receive her gift. She was so overcome she could hardly thank the teacher. A book so fine she had never imagined. There was a gift, too, for Sam, a Barlow knife with a shining red handle.

Weeks ago they had stopped driving Star to school, for Pa said it was too cold for her to stand out all day, and the three of them in the buggy was too much for Star to pull up the long steep hill through the mud.

Now, on the way home Serilda and Jeff carried all the other books and the dinner pail so that Katie could carry her gift.

"It has pictures of everything," Katie said blissfully as she stopped for the dozenth time and peeped inside. "Let's hurry to the log and sit down where we can really look at it."

"See if it says anything about thoroughbred horses," Serilda urged as they squeezed close together on the log, Katie in the middle.

"And bridges," Jeff said eagerly.

Katie ran her finger down the index . . . . "Bridges," she read proudly and turned to the page.

Jeff leaned over and stared intently. "Say, it does have everything." There was a picture of London Bridge, over the river Thames at London, England. Built in 1831, 54 feet wide and 928 feet long. A railroad suspension bridge over the Niagara River, two and one-half miles below the falls, built 1855. And a covered wooden bridge in Vermont, but a different type from the one almost in front of them.

Jeff looked from the picture of the Vermont bridge in the book, to the real bridge he knew so well, figuring out the difference, reading the text.

Serilda grew restless. "Don't look at the bridges all day, Jeff. Maybe Katie will let you read about them tonight. Katie, please, see if there is anything about horses."

Katie ran her finger down the index again and turned to the page. There were several pictures of horses. Underneath one it said "Thoroughbred," and Katie read aloud, "A breed established in England and descended from three great sires: the Byerly Turk, Darley Arabian and Godolphian Arabian. A son of Darley Arabian was imported to Virginia in

1730 and his descendants are known as Thoroughbreds. Since then many more have been imported
and their line of ancestors registered. It is primarily
a racing horse noted for its speed, but it is also finding favor as a pleasure horse. Swift on foot, highly
intelligent and strong of heart."

"That describes Star to a T," Serilda said with a
deep satisfying breath. "Katie, that is a wonderful
book."

Katie nodded, her eyes shining, as she smoothed
the pages with loving fingers. "If Maw could only
see it. She would be so mighty proud."

"Our ma and pa will be proud, too," Jeff said.
"Serilda and I have never brought home anything
that fine."

Serilda slid from the log and threw back her
shoulders.

"I'll have you remember, Jeff Shaw, that I brought
home something better than a book. A real, live blue-
ribbon horse named Star!"

Katie closed the book. "Not only once, she brought
her home twice, and the last time she had to run
her down!"

They laughed and started up the hill.

"Runty caused us a lot of worry and trouble and
got himself into a terrible mess, too," Serilda said
thoughtfully. "But I'm thankful he sold Star to
somebody that happened to come by this way, or I

would never have seen her again. I wonder why he let her go?"

"I think maybe he planned to ride her in races. Then after he rode her a few days, he decided she was too old, or her leg wouldn't stand it. Or maybe he just got scared after thinking over what he had done," Katie said.

"He should have gotten scared sooner," Jeff said shortly. "For in the letter our sheriff got from the one in St. Louis, Runty was wanted back in Ohio for horse stealing. And Pearson wasn't even his real name. Well, they caught him and the officers from Ohio came and took him back. He'll have a long time to be sorry."

"With a railroad and letter writing and the new telegraph that sends news so fast, folks can't expect to do bad things and not be found out," Katie said convincingly. "Even clear out West where they don't have these new things, their bad doings will catch up with them sometime."

Jeff and Serilda nodded in agreement.

Star was out in the pasture, walking slowly toward the barnlot gate when the children turned into the driveway. Serilda whistled and Star threw up her head and answered, quickening her pace. She was thick and heavy now with the unborn foal and she picked her way carefully over the rough spots and rocky places. Her mane and forelock had grown several inches and the walnut stain on her legs was gradually fading. By fall she should look like her old self again.

Serilda stood for a minute watching, loving her, wondering how she could ever wait until the middle of June for Star to have her colt. Wondering, too, if she would ever know if Star were a thoroughbred. Colonel Thompson should hear right soon, for it had been quite a spell since he had written last.

Katie and Jeff went into the house, but Serilda heard Pa coming in from the field where he had been plowing with Tib and Tony and she ran to meet him, telling him all about the last day of school and Katie's book.

"It tells all about bridges and thoroughbred horses," Serilda said, "and, Pa, it describes Star exactly."

Pa smiled, then his face sobered as he looked down at Serilda. "I've a little piece of news for you, Serilda. The Colonel was riding by today and came over in the field to tell me he had an answer to his last letter and there was no record on their books of a horse of Star's description. So I think Sam Wilson was just talking through his hat about Star being a thoroughbred, or maybe somebody fooled him because he couldn't read."

Serilda tried to keep back the tears as the disappointment swept over her. She had been so sure about Star.

"I think Colonel Thompson feels as bad as you do," Pa said as he took off the big bays' bridles and led them over to the trough to drink. "But there are lots of fine horses that aren't of pure blood, Daughter. Most of them aren't."

"I know, Pa," Serilda said brokenly. "That's why I wanted one. I thought maybe if Star's colt is a filly, sometime it could have a colt, too, and we could raise lots of thoroughbreds and have a regular horse farm."

"Pshaw! We can still raise horses." Pa smiled proudly at Serilda. "And no telling what might happen years from now."

CHAPTER 18

The Foal Is Born

APRIL AND May flew by, with Katie and Serilda helping Ma plant the garden and do the house cleaning, while Jeff worked in the fields with Pa. At corn planting all three of the children helped, dropping kernels of corn in the long rows Pa marked off across the field. It was a busy time.

Then it was June, with long, sunny summer days and soft warm showers. Across the cornfield, rows of green stalks grew lush and tall. Wheat began turning gold in the fields and oats were already being harvested.

Out in the pasture Star lazed away the days, eating the sweet, thick grass or dozing in the shade of the big oak, with now and then a trip, taking someone to the neighbors'. Lately she spent her nights in the big stall in the barn, knee-deep in fresh clean straw. Serilda counted off each day until only two were left before the colt was due. Then only one day was left.

Pa said best to keep Star in the barn all the time. Grandma said a queen couldn't have it any better

[163]

and Colonel Thompson stopped by to see how things were going.

But the day for the colt to come went by, and then the night, and still it was not born. "It will come in its own good time," Grandma told Serilda quietly. "The little thing is not quite ready and there is no hurrying nature. Star's not uneasy, look at her."

And Star wasn't worried as she stood with her head over the half door, watching the world around her, taking choice clover blooms and nibbles of apple that Serilda offered her. So another day passed and night came on with a low bank of clouds in the northwest, a warm sultriness in the air.

"The colt will come tonight," Grandma said prophetically. "Seems animals always pick a storm or a change in the weather to have their young."

At bedtime when Pa went to the barn with the children, Star was chewing on a wisp of hay and she looked at them in surprise, her brown eyes shining in the lantern light.

"You might as well go to bed and get some sleep," Pa said. "I can't tell for sure, but I believe she is going to put it off for another day."

"Listen, Serilda," Jeff whispered as they walked back to the house in Pa's long, dark shadow, "I'll tie a string onto my toe and hang it through the knothole and if you go to the barn in the night, pull on it and wake me."

"And wake me, too," Katie said as they undressed for bed.

It was hours later when Serilda woke from a restless sleep. A cool damp wind blew in the open window and for an instant a faint flicker of distant lightning outlined the room. Except for a gentle rain the storm had passed them by. Out in the chicken house a rooster crowed and Serilda knew it must be toward morning. A prickle of excitement raced over her. She nudged Katie awake and leaned close to her ear. "Shhhh, Katie, get up easy. Let's go see if the colt has come," she whispered.

Katie stirred sleepily. They got carefully out of bed and slipped their dresses on over their nightgowns. Tiptoeing to the kitchen, Serilda found the string and gave it a quick jerk, then another and another. Then they waited. It seemed a long time before they heard the squeak of Jeff's bed and the soft pad of his bare feet as he crossed the floor to the stairway.

Without a word they slipped out of the house and went toward the barn, Grover tagging along behind them. There was a faint light in the eastern sky, but it was dark inside the barn.

Star gave a soft, muffled nicker as they came to her stall. Then they heard another sound and stopped, holding their breath to listen. A soft swish-swish and new little snuffling noises. Serilda grabbed Jeff's arm and shook with excitement. She heard Katie take a quick breath beside her.

"It's been born," Serilda whispered. "She's licking it! I can hear it breathe!"

They went nearer and could see the dark shape of Star and in the thick shadows a smaller, darker form in the straw at Star's feet. Serilda spoke softly to Star, her voice trembling.

"I'll get the lantern." Jeff turned to go, but Serilda held his sleeve.

"Wait! Wait! Star might not want the lantern. It's coming light."

They hunched down in the straw listening to the soft sounds in the stall and the waking sounds of the world outside. Grover squeezed against them, his body shaking with the sight and smell of the new colt.

"It's like seeing it born," Katie said softly as the light filtered into the barn.

Serilda leaned closer, her heart pounding. "I can see it now! There's a star on its forehead, too, and one white foot!"

Star stopped her licking and gently nudged her baby. It lifted its head and tried to struggle to its feet, only to fall back on the straw. Star gave another lick and nudged again. Serilda started forward to help, but Jeff pulled her back. At last the colt was standing, long, knobby legs splayed far apart, like sticks propped under corners. Wisps of straw clung to its dark hair.

"It's a filly! A perfect little filly! When it's dry it'll be as black as its pa," Jeff cried out.

"Serilda, you've got your horse farm started!" Katie said gleefully.

Serilda couldn't speak. She felt weak with happiness.

They watched, breathless, as the little filly wobbled to Star's side and found the milk waiting for her. She made little sucking sounds of delight and switched her fuzzy tail. When she had her fill, she turned her head and looked at her new friends with brown eyes full of wonder, a white froth of milk around her mouth and on her short little whiskers.

Serilda caught her breath, then reached out to touch the filly's shining, silky hair, but Star nosed her hand away. Then Star made soft, loving sounds to her new baby as it tucked its legs under, curled up in the straw, and went to sleep. Star turned to them, her look as plain as words. "Being born, taking your first steps, eating your first meal, is hard work. Now let us rest."

They stepped outside into the rain-washed morning. Across the valley, Indian Hill was purple in the early light. There was a splendor in the air. Serilda took a long, deep, awesome breath.

"Now you have to name her. What's it going to be? Or do you know?" Jeff asked as they started toward the house.

Serilda looked at her brother with a secret, happy smile. "I've known for a long time," she said. "It is Locket."

"Locket!" Jeff and Katie gasped the name together.

Serilda nodded her head. "And when she is grown and has a family, I'll call her Lady Locket."

"It sure is a good name," Jeff said approvingly. "Sounds special, like a name for a thoroughbred."

"It is special," Serilda said softly.

"And who knows, maybe she is a thoroughbred," Katie said.

Serilda laughed and broke into a run. "Hurry! Let's tell everybody!"

In a few days Star and Locket were turned out into the pasture. The cattle were curious at first, but Star warded them off with sharp nips from her teeth when they got too near. Spring days had slipped into summer, with Locket growing like the wild morning glories along the rail fence.

She was as shiny and black as Grandma's Sunday dress, and the star on her forehead and her white foot were as clean as a snowflake. She learned to come when Serilda whistled, running ahead of Star to the pasture gate.

Before she was a month old Serilda was leading her around with a rope halter Pa had fashioned. Locket would keep her head close by Serilda's shoulder, sometimes rubbing her velvet nose on Serilda's sleeve.

Colonel Thompson stopped often to see her. He said she was the bonniest filly he had ever seen. He rubbed his hand along her straight little back and down her trim legs. Locket trembled with pleasure and rolled her big brown eyes while Serilda held her with the halter. Star, concerned, nickered softly.

"It is a shame," the Colonel said, "that she can't be registered. She has all the good marks of her sire and dam. It could be that Star is a thoroughbred and was never registered. Some people raise fine horses and are not interested in keeping up the papers. That might be the way it is with Star. Perhaps we'll never know." The Colonel sighed a bit sadly and mounted the Chief and rode away.

But Locket was not concerned about being registered. She was the happiest colt in the county. She raced over the pasture with Star, stretching her long slim legs. She learned to kick her heels high. She discovered the butterflies on the Jimson weeds. She shied from the shadows of low-flying birds. She learned to nibble grass with her new teeth and she would run up to Tib and Tony and stare into their big, patient faces, then wheel and race away.

Star, watching, would sometimes whinny reprovingly to Locket, and the filly would answer pertly in a high, squeaky little sound that would make Serilda and Katie double over with laughter.

But there were sad times, too, for Katie had not heard from her mother for months. Tales drifted back of Indian raids and the terrible hardships of wagon trains that had started for the west coast. Some families that had started came back, the horses or oxen sore and gaunt, the travelers tired and worn. Others that had left with loaded wagons returned on horseback with only a pack behind them. Sometimes in the night Katie talked in her sleep, saying her mother's name, and Serilda would shake her to break the dream. Every night when Pa read from the Bible and prayed, he asked God to keep watch over Katie's family, too. And so the days went by.

They had almost given up hope when the letter came, a long, wrinkled, hand-made envelope that Pa brought home one afternoon from the post office.

"Came clean from the Pacific Ocean to St. Joe by stagecoach and from there by train," Pa said as he handed the letter to Katie with a wide smile. "Feels thick. Must be full of news. And look what it cost to send it!"

Katie's smile was as wide as Pa's as she took the letter. "From Mrs. Samuel Wilson, Astoria, Oregon," Katie read shakily. "To Miss Katie Briggs, in care of Mr. William Shaw, near the Covered Bridge, Livingston County, Chillicothe, Missouri."

Jeff hopped up and offered his knife to slip under the flaps so that nothing would be torn. The envelope opened out into a square and there was writing on it too. There was a sheet of folded foolscap covered with the small, precise handwriting of Katie's mother, a little scrap of blue calico and a smaller, long, brown envelope.

Katie picked up the brown envelope and read, "To Miss Serilda Shaw, in care of her father William Shaw, near the Covered Bridge, Livingston County, Chillicothe, Missouri. Owner of Star, a sorrel mare with a large white star in forehead and four white stockings." She handed it proudly to Serilda.

Serilda beamed. "Well, it is mighty nice of your ma to remember me, too. But you've been waiting a long time. Read your letter first."

The whole family listened as Katie read her letter aloud, telling of the long, dangerous journey across the plains, the terrible hardships going over the mountains, but at last the beautiful Columbia River and then Astoria and the Pacific Ocean. Paw had filed on a homestead and built a one-room cabin a little way out from the settlement of Astoria. There were neighbors within half a mile. The boys were fine and often asked about Katie.

The last of the letter was especially for the Shaws. Maw wrote how much she appreciated what they were doing for Katie. How she prayed each night for them and loved them. Katie's eyes were misty when she finished, but there was peace and happiness on her face. She looked at Serilda. "Now read yours."

Jeff slipped his knife beneath the flap, but there was no letter inside, just a soiled, printed, legal-looking paper folded in thirds, with fancy letters on the outside at the top.

Serilda lifted it out wonderingly and looked at the letters and the writing underneath; then she suddenly gave a shout and held the papers high for everyone to see.

"It's Star's papers! She's a thoroughbred! She is! She is! Katie, your pa did tell the truth!" Serilda grabbed Katie and whirled around the room.

Pa stopped them and held out his hand. "Serilda, let me see it." Serilda gave it to him and squeezed up tight against him as he laid the paper on the table, reading the words on the back.

Certificate of Registration of RADIANT STAR, Reg. No. Owned by Irvin Sweeney
Bred by Irvin Sweeney
Signed: John R. Armstrong
Secy. of Registration

There was not a sound as Pa opened the sheet. Clipped to the inside were several long slips of paper, the top one fresh and new. Pa read it aloud.

TRANSFER OF OWNERSHIP

I, Samuel Wilson, do hereby transfer ownership of RADIANT STAR, a sorrel mare, with large white star in forehead and four white stockings, to Serilda Shaw.

October 1867

Signed: Samuel Wilson, X (his mark)

Witnessed by:

Everett Jones,
Astoria, Oregon.
September 1868

The name, Samuel Wilson, was in the fine writing of Katie's mother, but the heavy X was Paw's very own.

Underneath were other transfers of ownership, showing previous owners of Star, but none of them had been recorded in the next owner's name. This must be done before she was legally Serilda's. Down in the left-hand corner, set off by itself was this information:

Sex: Mare
Color: Sorrel, with sorrel mane and tail
Markings: Large white star in forehead and four
white stockings
Foaled: March 13, 1860, at Louisville, Ky.

[173]

Pa began tracing Star's history as it was shown, his rough finger following the names and numbers. Serilda read it, too.

Gray Light: Sire
Dawning Star: Dam

Then it went back through the years with all the names of her ancestors and their registration numbers and suddenly there it was! Serilda gasped as she read it, "Darley Arabian! Star a direct descendant of the Darley Arabian!" Awe-struck, they read it over and over, every word.

Serilda looked up at Katie, her face shining, "Oh, Katie, how can I ever, ever thank your mother? And your pa, too! I'll write them a letter this very night! And Star, let's go quick and tell her. And Locket!"

With trembling fingers Serilda took the papers and folded the envelope back around them, handing them to Pa for safekeeping. Then she hurried toward the door. Suddenly she stopped and whirled.

"Colonel Thompson has to know. Oh, Pa, tomorrow morning, can't Jeff and Katie and I hitch Star to the buggy and take the papers to show him? And couldn't we tie Locket's halter onto Star's bridle and let her go, too? She's big enough."

Pa looked across at Ma and Grandma and then back at Serilda, his brown eyes twinkling. "I think it would pleasure the Colonel very much," he said.

"You'll have to wear your Sunday clothes," Ma said quickly. "I'll press them right away. And Pa, Jeff needs a haircut. Can you do that now?"

"And the horses, don't forget to curry them, too."

Serilda streaked out of the door and toward the pasture, Jeff and Katie close behind. Star and Locket were grazing by the big flat rock. They threw up their heads and whinnied as the children and Grover came running toward them.

Serilda laid her face against Star's velvet nose and laced her fingers in her mane as Star nuzzled her shoulder.

"Radiant Star," she said with a little catch in her voice. "A registered thoroughbred, and real blood kin to the Darley Arabian! Oh, Star, I felt it all the time; now we can prove it! The papers came today!"

"And you're a thoroughbred, too," Jeff said proudly as Locket came up to him and snuffed his sleeve curiously.

"You'll have a new paper all your own," Katie said to the shining black colt, "with your name, Lady Locket, at the top. And who your Ma and Pa are and where you were born, and everything."

Locket gave a little snort and pawed with her white foot. Star stood quietly, her brown eyes alert and knowing, as she looked at the three loving faces before her, nickering softly when they finally left her to climb upon the big, flat rock.

After all the excitement, they were suddenly quiet as they looked out across their valley map, gold-tinged with autumn. They had seen the color change with every passing season, but the hills, the valley, the shine of Grand River would be the same forever. Now, the covered bridge was a part of it, too. Solid and staunch, it spanned the river, joining the roads, linking the settlers together. And the mill was there and the log house Grandpa had built so long ago and that was home for all of them, these were a part of their map, too.

Serilda thought of all that had happened in the two years since she sat here on the rock, watching for Jeff and Pa to come from Spring Hill with the timbers. She had been eleven then, now she was thirteen. She was growing up.

In her heart she could see the shining days ahead, days when Jeff would be building his bridges and Katie would be teaching school. Days when there would be other colts frolicking around Star, all of them proud and strong and swift. She gave a deep, contented sigh. With her finger she traced imaginary words on the flat surface of the rock . . .

SHAW'S HOME OF THOROUGHBRED HORSES

and at each end she drew a little outline of the covered bridge.